freak
magnet

Also by **ANDREW AUSEON**

Funny Little Monkey

Jo-Jo and the Fiendish Lot

freak
magnet

ANDREW AUSEON

HARPER **TEEN**
An Imprint of HarperCollinsPublishers

HarperTeen is an imprint of HarperCollins Publishers.

All poems written by Sarah Zogby and printed with permission.

Freak Magnet
Copyright © 2010 by Andrew Auseon
www.harperteen.com

Library of Congress Cataloging-in-Publication Data
Auseon, Andrew.
Freak magnet / Andrew Auseon. — 1st ed.
    p.   cm.
Summary: Two teenagers, both burdened by grief and loss,
find each other and gradually develop a strong connection.
ISBN 978-0-06-113926-0
[1. Interpersonal relations—Fiction. 2. Grief—Fiction. 3. Family
problems—Fiction. 4. Emotional problems—Fiction.] I. Title.
PZ7.A9194Fr 2010   2009030933
[Fic]—dc22   CIP
                                                          AC

Typography by Sasha Illingworth
10 11 12 13 14   LP/RRDB   10 9 8 7 6 5 4 3 2 1
❖
First Edition

For Saz
Remember us? I do.

ARIES
3/21–4/19

A good thing is right in front of you; you're not paying attention. Open your eyes.

FREAK

WHEN THE WORLD'S MOST BEAUTIFUL WOMAN WALKS INTO THE room, it's hard to keep from throwing up. At least that's how I felt when I first saw the girl in the doorway. I needed one of those little wax-coated paper bags you find in the seat-back pocket of an airplane; because I knew that I was looking at something pretty special.

She wore a black skirt, modest yet sexy, and white platform shoes without a single scuff on them. Her fingernails and toe-nails had been painted white—*white*—which made her skin seem all the browner, her long hair all the blacker. For a split second, her beautiful round face was scrunched up as if she'd smelled something weird, which wouldn't have surprised me, since it was a hundred degrees in DC that day, and human beings smell worse when they're heated up, and that place was packed.

It was the Monday after school let out for summer, and it was hellishly hot. My friend Edison and I sat in a window booth of a swanky café off the National Mall, picking the healthy parts out of our roast beef sandwiches. We would have preferred a greasy pizza from the hole in the wall two doors down, but the café had air-conditioning, and the man behind the counter wore rubber gloves, both of which were definite improvements over the other joint. Edison mumbled behind the growing pile of lettuce and vegetables he'd started on a napkin beside his plate. He was lost in his quest for something that once had a heartbeat. Me, I was lost in the girl.

As she walked across the café and stepped into the lunch line, I watched her distinctly mouth the words, "This place smells like pee," privately, under her breath, an act many people might have considered rude, even crude, but which I thought was charming. She was honest, and it's a fact that not enough people are really honest about how they feel. Not like me. With her first few words, I knew she and I had to meet. You could say she had me at "This place smells like pee."

I couldn't help but think of a supernova, the stellar explosion that occurs when a star either ceases generating energy or generates too much. Such a phenomenon throws everything out of whack. Data suggests that a single supernova releases enough radiation to outshine an entire galaxy—its light touches everything. Words associated with this event all indicate dramatic change: *release, collapse,* even *evolve.* And that's what happened to me: I wasn't the same after I saw her.

As Edison talked about what he was drawing—giant part-octopus aliens with suction cups for faces—I only half listened, hypnotized by the girl. I'd seen many women in my life, but none of them had ever kept my attention for more than a minute. She seemed to vibrate, in motion on a molecular level, so much energy below the surface. Yet she remained silent, waiting with her hands on her hips.

I interrupted whatever it was Edison was going on about, practically shouting over the AC unit that blasted in the window above us. "That girl is incredible." I decreed it. It was a proclamation because it was irrefutable fact.

Edison clammed up immediately. Then he looked around slowly for whatever woman I had pointed out. He was good at this, probably because he practiced it everywhere we went, like it was some sort of sport.

Once he found her, Edison dissected the girl from head to toe with his precision gaze, which is how he gathered information. Being an artist, he absorbed details from the world around him solely through his eyeballs. Sometimes he stared so hard, I almost expected to hear sucking noises, like how I imagined the part-octopus aliens might sound when they talked.

After a few seconds of close scrutiny, Edison turned back to his sandwich, unimpressed. "Meh," he said with a shrug. "I've seen better. She looks sort of evil, like a witch. Spooky."

I nodded and tapped my lip with a finger. "Funny you should point that out," I said. "I thought she looked a little like a hot zombie, and there are definitely similarities between witches and zombies."

"Yeah, well, similarities or not, neither is much of a compliment, Charlie."

"Says you," I told him, because I certainly meant my zombie comment to be nice.

I'd lost all interest in my lunch fixings. "I should talk to her," I said, flicking a slice of tomato off the table onto the floor.

Edison stopped with soda halfway up his straw, and he looked at me. "What?"

"I should talk to her, you know."

"Why?"

"To tell her that she's the most beautiful girl I've ever seen in my life."

"That's not the best idea you've ever had," he said. "You have a tendency to go all *Charlie* around strangers. Remember when you showed those physicists your psoriasis at last year's National Science Foundation mixer? You nearly got us tasered. Besides, it's weird to say that to someone. She'll probably call Homeland Security or something. Black helicopters will snatch us up before we hit the sidewalk." He burped and rolled his eyes. "That's if the food poisoning doesn't off us first. Wow. I think that roast beef was still breathing."

I pushed my plate away from me across the table, arms crossed. "You see. *That's* the problem."

"What's the problem?" Edison eyed me suspiciously.

"*That!* That for some reason it's weird if I want to tell a girl she's beautiful. For some reason it's totally *insane*, even though, and I'd put money on it, she'd appreciate that I went out of my way to say it. Think about it. Who in their right mind *wouldn't* want to walk into a café at one in the afternoon and get told that they are the best-looking person a slightly awkward but reasonably attractive complete stranger has ever seen?"

He stared at me, the soda sliding up and down his straw. "I wouldn't, for one."

"Well, in your case it would never even come up."

"True," he said, sighing. "I may have money, but it can't buy me love."

"You know what I'm saying?" I asked, fishing for the response that I wanted.

"You lost me around 'insane,'" said Edison. "That's usually when you lose me." He sighed. "Stick to the stars,

Charlie. You don't do so well when you're here on Earth with the rest of us."

"What's the *big* deal?" I said, and I threw my arms out, accidentally knocking the salt-and-pepper shakers to the floor. Dropping to my knees, I snatched up the little plastic doodads before they could roll away. I was always doing stuff like that, knocking things over, walking into walls, accidentally shouting in public . . . or church.

Even with my head under the table, I kept talking. "It's a *good* thing. If I wanted to go up to a stranger and look him in the eye and say, 'Hey, man, you are one ugly bastard. I have never seen an uglier bastard,' then that's one thing. You know? But to tell someone she looks—"

"Like the undead?" interrupted Edison.

"*Exactly!*" I'd started shifting into frantic mode—"to go all Charlie," as Edison called it. My voice became higher and faster, and I started to trip over words. "I'm making a statement here."

"A statement?"

"Like a fortune cookie. A candy heart."

"Explain," said Edison, leaning in, interested at last.

I watched the girl out of the corner of my eye. The little guy behind the counter handed her a cup of hot coffee that steamed as she took it, and she headed to the cream-and-sugar kiosk. Hot, steaming coffee on a hundred-degree day; I loved it.

I looked away. "Whoever that girl is, wherever she came from, and wherever she's going, she'll always have my compliment. She can file it away with all the other things that make her smile. Then, one day, when she's lower than she's ever been, like, maybe she gets dumped by her boyfriend, or someone forgets her birthday, or she fails a biology quiz on helper B cells . . . *Boom!* I'll be there. She'll remember what I said, and she'll feel good. She'll remember *me*."

"You make a good case," said Edison. "But I still think it's a bad idea."

"Why is it a bad idea? It's a *good* case!"

He shook his head and smiled, cleaning off his glasses with the front of his shirt. A shelf of brown curls bounced around on his forehead. "Because people don't do that sort of thing, Charlie."

I tapped the tabletop with a finger. "Which is exactly why I *should* do it."

"Charlie, you're only in town for another couple months. Leave it alone. Why make a first impression when that's all you'll ever get?"

"You just answered your own question."

Sighing, he popped his glasses back on. "Fine, you probably should do it."

"Wait, what?"

He leaned back in his wheelchair with a squeak, collar fluttering in the arctic AC breeze. "Charlie, after ten years I think I know you pretty well, and don't take this the wrong way, but you sometimes develop what I like to call a 'reality problem.' You occasionally live in a bizarre imaginary bubble of your own design. So when you ask me if you should do something, I usually resist only as long as I feel is customary."

"And why is that?"

"Because I know you're going to do whatever you want anyway," he said. "So why fight the inevitable?"

I pointed at him, pleased. "Right! Now *that's* what I'm talking about!"

"Whatever," he said with a shrug.

Slurping a mouthful of soda, I slammed my hands down on the table. "This is it!" I got up out of the booth.

Predictably, because nothing ever works out for me the way it should, the girl was gone, vanished in a cloud of five-dollar cappuccino steam.

It knew it couldn't end like that. I didn't know why, but the stars seemed to be aligning for once; I could feel a change occurring, a release, a collapse, an expulsion . . . an evolution. I'd be damned if I'd let a moment that golden get away when I had such long legs, not to mention three Cokes worth of caffeine pumping through my system. So I dashed for the doorway, where the throb of summer heat pumped in from the street like a pulse.

Studies suggest that during its explosion, a supernova releases as much energy as our sun can emit over its entire lifespan. I knew the feeling.

"Good luck!" called Edison after me. "Don't forget to hold your breath when she maces you!"

MAGNET

"HERE'S MY CARD," THE STRANGER SAID, HANDING ME A RECT-angle of paper he'd undeniably printed on his home computer. A picture showed a melting candle sitting on a skull. A title read, "Daniel Diamond, Foreseer." The heavy ink made the ends of the paper curl.

"Thank you, sir," I said. "I'll definitely check it out."

His puffy coat squeaked as he tugged a wool cap low over his brow. I didn't remind him that it was a hundred degrees outside. "Remember," he said, pointing at me, "avoid the color orange."

"Can do," I assured him.

Then, with a whoosh of AC, the man disappeared into the din of the café—for the third time in five minutes.

People can be so strange.

Sun reflected in the puddles of Seventh Street. A few stray raindrops struck the patio table umbrellas. They fell popping to the concrete. Around me, a steady stream of customers entered and exited the café. Even in the post-thunderstorm swelter, the crowd never thinned. People need coffee.

I hurried across the crosswalk into the National Gallery's Sculpture Garden. Daniel Diamond, Foreseer, was a typical catch for a Saturday at one P.M. No matter how sensitive his skills of precognition, he couldn't have predicted our meeting. Not before I did. When you attract weirdos like I do, your guard is always up.

Everyone is capable of at least fifteen minutes of insanity. Some are just better at keeping it from bubbling to the surface. I'm okay with letting those like Daniel Diamond pitch me their crazy. Once they get it out of their systems, they move on. He was harmless. It was painless. I was free. (Well, until the next one.)

There was one thing I never understood though: Why would you want to talk to a total stranger in the first place? People are work. They're tiring. They hurt you when they don't even mean to. They make you doubt yourself. And more often than not, they go away. Getting close to people is like building a city on a fault line. Why would you ever do so on purpose?

"HELLO!"

Some weirdo in the garden was shouting. But I wasn't in the mood to talk to someone else, not so soon after Daniel Diamond. So I walked on. I didn't even know if the shout was for me. Did it matter?

"HEY! YOU! GIRL WITH THE SHOES! GIRL WITH THE PLATFORM SHOES!"

That was it. I glanced over a shoulder, searching for the person attached to the voice. Doing so, I nearly collided with a pair of African men in flowered shirts. I got out of their way just in time but bumped against a stone pillar along the path. "Damn!" I grunted. I hated this freak already, and I hadn't even laid eyes on him.

"GIRL WITH THE HOT COFFEE! HEY, HOT-COFFEE GIRL!"

I stopped at last, swiveling around on one heel. "*WHAT?*"

Much to my surprise, I found a boy staring back at me. He was my age.

I stood frozen on the path. A sculpture of a giant rabbit loomed over me. Fir trees rustled in a summer breeze, like little whispers. Totally surreal.

The guy was a psycho, sort of. (Cute, though, if you're into that sort of thing—foaming-at-the-mouth crazy.) He was tall, really tall, with whitish blond hair. His icy blue eyes seemed to tremble. They went well with the general jitteriness of his movements, like those of an overcaffeinated bird. He seemed to constantly twitch with nervous energy. It suited him.

"Are you talking to me?" I said, hand on my chest.

"Yeah," he managed, out of breath.

"Why?" I asked. "What do you want?"

"I just wanted to tell you something."

"That I have platform shoes and hot coffee?" I asked, oozing sarcasm. "Thanks, I'm aware."

"No," he said. "But the shoes do make it look like you have exceptionally long legs, like you're on stilts or something. Of course, you probably wouldn't even notice that unless you're *really* looking."

A chill ran through me. I crossed my arms and hugged myself. "And you were *really* looking?" I asked.

"Well, *yeah*," he said, laughing. "My friend and I were in that café you just left. You probably didn't even notice us. I watched you the whole time you were in line."

A woman pushed a stroller between us, and I blinked, just once. It was enough to break our gaze. I wasn't sure what this guy wanted from me, but I'd had enough. Pulling my purse closer to my body, I turned away. "Well, the next time you notice me, keep it to yourself. Okay?"

I hurried off, speed walking up the path, my chin raised to the sun, eyes forward.

He stumbled after me, of course. "Wait. Listen," he called. Why didn't this goofball just go away, leave me alone? "I'm not crazy or anything. Honest. And I didn't mean to scare you. I only wanted to tell you that I think you're the most beautiful girl I've ever seen. That's okay, right?"

Something sparked in me, and damn it, I hesitated. Again, I turned on a heel and stared into his face. I don't know why I did it. His eyes glowed in the sun, textured blue, like feathers.

"Are you insane?" I asked, seriously hoping for an answer.

His brow crinkled. He was actually considering it. "I don't think so."

"What do your friends say?"

Again, the crinkling brow. "I only have one."

"Well, hold on to him," I said, not wanting to hear more (but also, maybe, wanting to). "Now go away."

"Why?" he asked. "What did I do?" He seemed genuinely confused about why I might be unnerved.

"Just leave me alone," I said.

"But it's a compliment. It's a *good* thing," he insisted. "*Please*."

"I'm trying to be *nice*."

We were speaking two different languages. So I decided to act instead: with a swirl of my black skirt, I made my escape. Off I walked toward Constitution Avenue, my shoes making Frankenstein *clunks* on the pathway.

Later, weirdo.

FREAK

EVEN AFTER SHE'D WALKED AWAY, I COULD STILL SMELL HER—
floral, powdered. On a hot city day clogged with bus exhaust
and BO, she was a flower that refused to wilt in the weather.

I caught one last sight of her in the distance, a red ribbon
hanging from her long black hair. It reminded me of the curling skin of a peeled apple. In all her dark clothes, she sort of
reminded me of a serial killer, but in a good way, the kind of
killer who charms you into joining her murder spree. Then,
like that, she was gone in the growing tourist crowds.

Grumbling, I dropped down on a bench and tried to shake
off the gloom of my failure. I found myself doing this a lot in
my life, staving off disaster at every turn. It isn't easy; you've

got to practice resilience, build up a thick skin over time and over tragedy. You've got to become bulletproof.

As I always did when I felt low, I tried to remember back to some of the worst moments in Superman's life, those that required his utmost Kryptonian strength and endurance. For example, during the *Crisis on Infinite Earths* story line, Supergirl dies when saving Superman's life from an alien monstrosity called the Anti-Monitor. This loss shook the Man of Steel to his very core. How did he get through it? Well, in typical comic-book fashion, all events involved in the crisis were wiped from memory, as if Supergirl had never even existed. How convenient for our hero.

I took the cue and tried to imagine that I hadn't seen the girl in the café and that I hadn't chased her down howling like a madman. Maybe Edison was right, and maybe some things are better left unsaid, undone, uncomplicated. I had enough complexity in my life and didn't need to deal with one more variable. Still, the girl had been beautiful, and interesting, and a little prickly, which isn't attractive to everyone but I think is super hot.

Feeling somewhat better, I gazed at the activity around me. I hadn't even bothered to notice the garden, the people. I so often do that: forget to see what's right there. I'm always pressing my face to an eyepiece or sticking my nose in a book. It's easy to forget the billions of other people inhabiting all

197 million square miles of good old planet Earth. I took a deep breath and focused. I was a naturally happy person. I was all about optimism. Of course, it's hard to concentrate when your crotch itches so badly.

It was the tights I wore under my clothes—they tended to bunch. They weren't exactly summer fashion, either, but I needed to wear them, always, especially on days when the world seemed out to thwart me.

I unbuttoned my top button and touched the large emblem underneath: a red *S*. Two months. Two months and I'd be gone, far away. All of this would be behind me.

He may be an alien, but I bet even Superman hates Mondays.

MAGNET

MY HEART THUMPED SO HARD I COULD SEE THE VEINS ON THE BACK of my hand tremble. I walked on, trying to forget the past and focus on the present. Who was that kid? Was he for real? Was it a joke? (It hadn't felt like a joke. From the looks of it, that kid couldn't have been more serious. That was the creepiest part.)

Closing my eyes, I tried to distance myself from the moment by thinking of something else. I floated up, up, and away. Like Mary Poppins on her magic umbrella. This usually worked. I was always blowing away bad memories like yesterday's newspaper—the smaller ones, anyway. Some memories are too heavy.

Clear again, I stood outside the Sculpture Garden and let

the hot DC wind blow over me. It was mostly car exhaust and grit from the National Mall. Still, when a breeze shows up on a hundred-degree day, you take what you can get.

That was the truth of my existence. Despite my evasion of Sculpture Garden Guy, the same thing would probably happen again in a few minutes. Or at the next intersection. Or even before I reached the end of the block. I was one of those: I was a magnet, a walking spiderweb for the soul-sucking mosquitoes of freakdom.

Here's how it worked: A guy approaches seemingly from out of nowhere. It's always a guy. And it's always the guy in the room who you want near you the least. As soon as you accidentally make eye contact, he latches on for dear life. All the while every other chick in the room watches, thinking, "Thank god for that poor bitch. She's taking the heat for all of us." (That's what I like about women: we stick together. Ha.) I'm like the sacrificial virgin, only without the virgin part.

I don't necessarily blame the guys who come up to me. Most of the time they're just needful, lonely; and I, of all people, can understand that feeling. Everyone wants to connect. It's a pull, a force of nature. Still, why do they always want to connect with *me*?

I walked down Madison Drive to where my car was parked at a meter. My sister Maggie and I had planned to meet at one, but it was one fifteen. Maggie was nowhere to be seen. Earlier, she'd made some joke about going to the Vietnam

Memorial to find vulnerable older men. More than likely she had hiked to Chinatown to find a comic-book shop.

It was that time of the month again. She expected her monthly red visitor, though I wasn't sure which one, Daredevil or the Flash. (All those guys in tights looked the same to me.)

I climbed into my car, shut the door, and started the engine. The blast of AC was nothing but hot air. Outside, tourists passed, fanning themselves with maps. I knew the guy who sold them, Dmitri. He hocked junk at the top of the Metro escalators. Things like city guides and pencil sharpeners shaped like the Lincoln Memorial. Cars honked in traffic. I sat quietly, wilting and chewing my nails.

I waited. The car creaked even though it wasn't moving. It was the plastic dashboard changing shape in the heat. All the activity outside made the near silence inside suffocating. But I couldn't go back out there. Not with all those people.

In preparation for the drive, I popped off my shoes. Then I took my driving glasses out of the glove compartment. I hesitated putting them on, pondering my reflection in the rearview mirror. I looked better without them.

At a young age I'd decided that I would be much better looking *without* certain things—*without* glasses, *without* beauty marks, and especially *without* the bump in my nose. I made a face at myself. (Stupid Arab profile—I looked like a political cartoon.)

The strange boy's words came back to me as I set my bare feet on the hot dashboard. Had he really said I was beautiful? I thought back to the Sculpture Garden. I've had my fair share of freak encounters but never had someone pursue me like that before—at a dead sprint, screeching. I might have been flattered. If I hadn't been so damn spooked.

With a thud, I dropped my glasses back into the glove compartment. I took out something else instead: a small green and white composition book. I called it my Freak Folio. I pulled off the fat pink rubber band that held the pages shut. Then I took the pen from its worn groove along the binding. Turning to page forty-seven, I wrote:

Perhaps I should set booby traps
in all my well-plotted paths.
How else to keep them out.
This one ran at me as if he'd seen a ghost—
as if he were a sniveling kid
who just discovered I was his mother
unvanishing from the grocery aisle
after he'd wandered away.

I could blame the sticky heat,
mistaken identity, my ravishing beauty.
But it's all a lie.

As I wrote, a sense of relief spread through me. I didn't feel panicked anymore. I stopped and read what I'd written. Sure, the quality was more *Chicken Soup for the Soul* than *Ulysses*, but it did the trick. The boy from the garden was fading.

I snapped the rubber band around the pages and shoved the journal back into the glove compartment. I slid down in my seat, watching the people on the Mall. Sweat soaked through my shirt and made the plastic cushion sticky.

All was right with the cosmos. No one could touch me.

ARIES
3/21–4/19

Take care of yourself. Nurture your own growth and find happiness.

FREAK

"TEN BUCKS I CAN CLEAR THE CASE OF JIFFY POP!"

"I'll take that bet," said Little Tommy. "Will you take a check with Spider-Man on it?" Jelly bracelets gleamed on his girlish wrists.

"I take all forms of payment," I said, raising a finger. "Now who's in?" The four of us—my fellow Customer Service Associates Lawrence and Arnold, Little Tommy, and me—stood beside a crate of hollow chocolate Easter bunnies that had been on sale for a solid fourteen months straight. Originally priced at ten dollars, they were now a very reasonable ninety-nine cents.

Lawrence sneezed into the shoulder of his red vest as he handed me the two-by-four I'd taken from the

27

stockroom. "I'm in."

"You're a good man," I said, slowly unloading the crate of shampoo onto the floor, one bottle at a time. "The world needs more guys like you, given you bump up the personal hygiene a notch."

"There is no way you're ever going to make that distance," said Little Tommy. "That shampoo has the consistency of caulking."

"Listen," I said, lecturing, "it's important to approach everything you do with a positive attitude. If you're already convinced of your eventual failure, why put forth the effort in the first place?"

"Little Tommy's right," said Lawrence as he sniffed loudly, pressing a knuckle against his nose. "You're just going to make a mess." The poor, paunchy kid was one of those people with allergies so bad that they didn't even need triggers, as though he were allergic to life itself.

"There is no mess yet," I said. "There is only the opportunity for greatness. Were the Wright brothers concerned with making messes? Thomas Edison? Friedrich Bessel?"

"Who?" Little Tommy asked.

"You're squirting shampoo bottles for distance," said Arnold, rolling his eyes. "And I'll tell you again. Don't do it."

"Just stand back," I said. Dusting off the knees of my pants, I stood up to my full six-foot-four and gazed down at the awesomeness of what I'd created. Twelve lawn gnomes stood around waiting for placement on the Aisle Two shelves. I'd turned all of them to face me, and they formed the perfect line of spectators for my experiment, a row of potbellies and rosy cheeks.

I worked at Family Friends, the drugstore that claimed it was in "everyone's neighborhood," although I think there were only four locations, all of them in northern Virginia. I pretty much had the same title as the other three guys, "Customer Service Associate," which was nothing more than a collection of odd jobs. One minute you could be sprinkling sawdust on baby barf, and the next you could be stuck in the one-hour photo lab, breathing toxic fumes as you hallucinated about doing something better, like, say, sprinkling sawdust on baby barf. I had only worked at the store for one week and was already itching to turn in my red vest and smiley-face name tag. To say I get bored easily is an understatement.

Uncapping two different plastic bottles of shampoo, I set them on the floor alongside each other. I bridged them with my two-by-four of wood. "The key to success," I declared, "will be the even distribution of force and weight." I squinted at the arrangement on the floor.

Little Tommy snickered but then covered his mouth with his hand.

"Don't do it," said Arnold. "You'll have to clean it up."

"I must know how the products we peddle perform under

rigorous testing. You know what I always say, 'An informed customer is a better customer.'"

"I've never heard you say that," said Lawrence.

"Charlie, quit now while you're ahead. For once," said Arnold.

I stepped up to the board. "What's the point of doing anything if you're not going to take it seriously?" I said.

"Well, it's *your* job to lose," said Arnold, averting his eyes.

"Yes, it is," I answered. The tape measures were drawn. The gnomes looked on. I was ready.

I teetered on my tiptoes, ready to jump, when a customer rounded the corner of Aisle Two.

She was young, and pretty, and pregnant, carrying a belly as big around as a bowling ball in her nervous hands. The four of us stared. We must have looked terribly shocked and pathetic in our scarlet vests, like a barbershop quartet that had fallen on hard times. The woman wore a trendy maternity outfit that was suited to her body, making what could have been a potentially frightening figure into one you just wanted to cuddle.

"Excuse me," she said.

"You want to watch?" I asked. "I'm going for distance, but I'll settle for style."

The woman opened her mouth to answer but didn't speak.

Arnold was quick to save the day. "Good morning," he said, sliding the tone of his voice from scolding screech to false warmth, a change anyone who knew him could detect a mile away. "Can I help you find something?"

Ever since I'd known him, meaning one week, Arnold had treated me like I needed constant reining in, and whenever we were together it was his job to be my handler. I don't know about most people, but I don't enjoy being treated like a bull in a china shop, especially by a kid with a snaggletooth.

"I was wondering about baby formula?" said the woman, her eyes still lingering on the floor, where my shampoo experiment had been interrupted in the name of customer service.

"No problem," said Arnold with a friendly smile. He was friendly only when he needed to be, when it was expected of him or when he could get something out of it. That wasn't a way to be friendly. Friendliness came from inside, like decency, or love, or the ability to speak a foreign language. No. I could not allow Arnold this victory. It went against everything I stood for.

"No, I got it!" I said, and hurried over.

Arnold glared at me, but I resisted his evil pull, and since he's smaller than me, and a coward, he relented.

"Come with me, please," I said, politely escorting the woman fetus-first past the stacks of summer badminton sets and flavored water to Aisle Five, the baby aisle. Over my shoulder I saw my three coworkers wander back to their chosen positions. Arnold, poor Arnold, picked up the two shampoo bottles and placed them back on the shelf with hundreds of others just like them, arranging the rows so flawlessly that in a second I couldn't spot the ones we'd taken down.

I was feeling like an incredibly helpful employee when the woman and I reached the end of Aisle Five. "Personally, Aisle Five is my favorite aisle," I told her, rocking back on my heels.

"Why is that?" asked the woman.

"Well," I said, gazing at the shelves overflowing with bright baby packaging, "you got your swim diapers, your sippy cups, a few different styles of novelty cell phones. Everything a baby needs." The woman smiled at me as I continued. "It has a positive, candy-colored kid vibe. Although I never really go down this aisle, since I would never buy anything in it, and honestly, just thinking about having children terrifies me. Kids are a major drain on our natural resources. It would probably be better to adopt one of the millions of orphans living in the American foster-care system. I mean, why bring another person onto an already overcrowded planet? That's just nuts."

"I see," the woman said. Her face had suddenly tightened into a tense web of wrinkles.

I began to backpedal, fast.

"I didn't mean to offend you or anything, really," I said. "I just don't want to have kids. You know, for me. I find them kind of annoying. Plus, I could never bring a baby into a world that's only got a few billion years or so left, and that's if it doesn't get bashed by some stray asteroid or something. But, hey, that's just my personal choice. I'm sure your baby will definitely make the most of the opportunity."

The woman lifted one hand to the side of her face. "I have to go," she said, starting to turn toward the door.

"Wait! What do you need? I can help." I practically threw my body down in her path. My voice had risen to near-screeching levels. "I know more about what we sell than any of the other guys in here do, I swear."

Breathing heavily, she stopped, fingers massaging the massive bump drooping over the waist of her black pants. "It's awfully rude to say something like that," she said, her voice icy. "Children are a blessing."

"I know!" I said. "Honest! Don't listen to a word I say. Please, I didn't mean anything by it." I had to prove I wasn't as inept as Arnold said. I had to keep my big mouth shut and make a sale.

The woman sighed, her chest heaving. "It's okay," she said. "Let's try again. I'm looking for a kind of Enfamil baby formula, but I don't see it on the shelf."

"Well," I said, trying to sound authoritative like Arnold,

"we actually only carry a few brands, because we have limited shelf space for formula, and diapers sell so much better. And unfortunately we're sold out of Enfamil at the moment."

"Oh," she said, a friendly smile curling up in the corners of her mouth. "Well, thanks anyway."

"Sure," I said. "Glad I could help." Then, before I could stop myself, I added, "And you might want to forgo formula altogether."

"Why's that?"

Since she asked: "Breast-feeding is better for the baby."

A slight redness came into her cheeks. "Well, that would be my business," she said, voice wavering.

"From what I've read, there have been a number of reported cases of tainted baby formula both in the U.S. and abroad," I said. "They're usually contaminated with melamine cyanurate, which can cause kidney failure."

"Is that true?"

"I think so," I said. And, because I've never practiced the "quit while you're ahead" method of conversing, I added, "Do you really want to feed your kid something that's used as a fire retardant?"

The pregnant woman glared at me. I waited, clenching and unclenching my fists, thinking for a second that I might have a shot at turning this whole thing around.

"Something is seriously wrong with you," she said.

"Wait!" I said, confused. "I'm trying to be helpful."

"You're not helpful," she said. "You need help." Then she walked down the aisle and out the sliding front doors, clutching her unborn child even closer than before.

I'd done it again. Epic fail.

Little Tommy drifted over from where he'd been tearing photos out of men's interest magazines and stuffing them into the pockets of his jeans. He held a price gun in one hand, his eyes beady under a mop of hair. "What did you say?" he asked.

"I just thought she should know," I said. "I was trying to be honest."

Shrugging, Little Tommy shot me in the shoulder with his gun. "I guess people dig denial," he said. "Who knew?"

Fifteen minutes later, I slouched in the squeaky chair in front of Mr. Pastore's desk, a seat that I had gotten pretty used to in my single week of employment. At Family Friends, you screw up and you find your butt planted in Mr. Pastore's squeaky chair. It didn't matter if you were family or not, friend or not. The employer promised equal-opportunity reaming. Even Arnold couldn't cut a break, and he was Mr. Pastore's son.

The manager's office consisted mainly of a small metal desk and a metal chair, the pad of which had been worn down paper thin. A whiteboard on the wall detailed the comings and goings of the store's employees, while the rest of the decor was classic cinder block graced with a few cobwebbed Saint Patrick's Day decorations that had never been taken down.

As I waited for my punishment, I pored over Washington DC's recent star figures in the tiny black logbook I kept tucked in my hip pocket. Most nights, I sat by my bedroom window, a cup of hot jasmine tea on the windowsill, telescope precisely aligned, and created long tables called ephemerides, which are used to determine the location of astronomical bodies at a given time. It was probably my biggest hobby, other than the unhealthy obsession with everything Superman.

Over the last few months I'd been tracking something (and I call it a *thing* only because I had no idea what it was) and had the ridiculous, nay, the presumptuous suspicion that it was a comet—an *undiscovered* comet. This wasn't the first time I'd jumped to such a conclusion. However, I tried not to think too much about what had happened when I last mistakenly identified a small celestial body. Several observatory directors have since unlisted their phone numbers.

I could look at the sky forever. There's always something to look at, to notice. You're reminded that nothing stops, not even when it feels like everything else in your life has ground to a halt. Our world will keep turning, revolving, long after we're gone.

By the time I heard Mr. Pastore's footsteps in the long

basement hallway, I had gotten lost in the following figures, checking the numbers of my object against those my computer had generated for the previous nights:

Name	Right Ascension	Declination	Altitude	Start Time
Dorothy	00:12:23	+30:05:00	-09:05	A.D. 2009-Jun-11
				00:00:00.0000 UT

Mr. Pastore stood outside; just his hands and the tips of his shoes were visible in the tall, thin gap between the doorway and the wall. He stood at the coffee vending machine dropping in change. Each coin made a clink before it rolled around the insides. He cleared his throat a few times—a lifetime smoker—and hitched up his pants.

I concentrated as long as I could before the door opened. It was a good thing I had my logbook with me to direct all my nervous energy. Last visit to the boss's office, I'd been so bored waiting I'd stapled my shoes to the floor. That had earned me an entirely separate appointment in the chair of doom.

Mr. Pastore entered. "Hey, Charlie," he said, walking in carrying his sad excuse for a coffee. The way he wheezed my name suggested that it was almost too much physical activity for him to manage. He stood at his chair and evaluated his approach before carefully sitting with a loud groan.

"Hi, Mr. P.," I said. "How's the biz? Are things looking

good for the Family Friends these days?" I was stalling, hoping he'd forget why I'd been sent down into the recesses of the strip mall and put off unemployment for one more day.

"Sure, sure," he said, lost in thought.

"Glad to hear it. This job is good stuff. Thanks again for making it happen."

"Sure, sure," he said again.

I shifted in my chair, trying without success not to squeak. "So what can I do for you today?" I asked.

Mr. Pastore held his coffee with a bony, clawlike hand, and stared off into space, sipping. This meant he stared at the faded maroon poster entitled "Maui Sunset" that he'd probably hung five years ago on his first day as manager. To him, the poster must have passed for a window. "I'm sorry to do this during your shift, Charlie," he said, "but we need to chat." He looked so much like Arnold, it was hard not to notice—for me, anyway. They could have been two versions of the same guy, one of whom had traveled in a time machine to visit the older, balder version of his future self.

"No worries," I said. "We're not exactly crowded." Mr. Pastore rarely entered the store itself, so you needed to remind him about life there. Whenever it got busy on the sales floor, he'd vanish below the surface into his underground tunnel system and stay there until it was safe to reemerge, like some kind of shriveled-up prairie dog.

"Well, if things get busy, the other boys can handle it," he said.

I sat up in my chair with a truly obscene squeak. "No offense," I said, "but the only way your boys out there know how to run this place is right into the ground."

Mr. Pastore's blank, default expression shifted a little, and he sort of smiled. "I think they'll manage okay if you're gone for five minutes. They certainly did for a whole year before you showed up."

"Don't bet on it," I said. "You should count your fruit smoothies when you go back out there. Lawrence has what we like to call 'a problem.'"

"Listen, Charlie," he said, "this isn't about Arnold and Lawrence."

"Then that's your first mistake," I pointed out, knowing that I was probably just making things worse. No matter how hard I tried, I never struck the right balance with other people. No calculation can successfully predict their behavior, or mine.

Mr. Pastore sighed. He was the kind of guy who sighed a lot, who sat hunched in a chair with holes in the soles of his shoes, and who sported a tie that he wore so often, the creases from the knot were permanently pressed into the fabric. I felt bad for him, because he was way too young to be trapped in a dead-end job. Of course, he was also too old to go out there and expect to find a better one.

"Charlie," he said, "I gave you this job as a favor to your dad, because I know you need some extra cash before you head out for . . ."

"Chile," I finished for him. Mr. Pastore and my dad had played high school football together back in prehistoric times, when mammoths roamed the wasteland and telephones had cords.

"Right, Chile." Reaching up, he tugged the single clump of hair that remained on his gleaming little skull, and after moving slightly, it immediately snapped back into position. "Sounds like you've got quite the year ahead of you with that astronomy stuff. Frankly, most of it is over my head; but I understand that you're about to take a big step, and I appreciate that."

"Thanks," I said, and meant it.

He went on. "You are a great kid, with great intentions. But customer service isn't a science. It's more of an art. And if you keep acting up, I'm going to have to take you off the sales floor."

Then everything fit together to make perfect sense—his line of questioning, the overly squeaky chair, his making me wait for an eternity as he purchased vending machine coffee. I was being set up. "You're going to fire me, aren't you?" I asked.

A fist of cold fear knocked the wind out of me. I clasped my hands in front of me and squeezed as hard as I could to keep from flipping out. My fingers turned from white to purple. I knew my job could be performed perfectly well by a monkey on tranquilizers, but I didn't want to lose it. No. I needed the money. Without it, I couldn't leave the country.

"I'm not going to fire you, Charlie," said Mr. Pastore. The long, flat fluorescent fixture overhead popped and gave off a smell of fried plastic. "But if you're going to engage customers, you're going to need to calm down. Just do your job. Serve the customer. Answer the question. Simple is easy. Small talk is difficult, unpredictable."

"Serve the customer. Answer the question. Simple is easy." Like a parrot, I flawlessly regurgitated the information. "I can do that. No problem."

The panic must have shown in my eyes, because Mr. Pastore stopped slowly rocking in his chair and made eye contact for the first time since he'd started talking. But once I met his stare, I looked away, focusing on the ripples and cracks in the concrete. I thought about how I was going to do a better job at work. How I would rise through the ranks of the company. I could do it. I knew I could. I'd show them all.

"How's your mom, Charlie?"

My gaze shifted from the floor to my hands. They lay

useless in my lap, like a couple of unattached prosthetics. I couldn't feel them. It was as if they belonged to someone else. "She's doing okay," I said.

"Good. I'm glad." He smiled. "Dorothy was always a fighter."

His use of *was* took me by surprise. There was no *was* about my mom. She was very much an *is*.

Mr. Pastore leaned forward in his chair, elbow on the table. "Charlie, I know you're not interested in a career in retail or anything, and I know that dealing with people all the time isn't exactly in your skill set." Boy, did he have that right. "So my suggestion to you, one man to another, is to put your head down, do your job, and avoid situations that could potentially cause problems." He wrung his hands over his large, flat desktop calendar. "Take control, all right?"

"Control," I said.

"Think you can manage that?"

"Oh, I can manage."

What he didn't know was that I could do anything, because I had found my superpower. I wore it then, during our conversation. Although I'd left the cape at home.

It wasn't easy being weak all the time, needing a crutch to get through everyday life. Even Superman gets a taste of this kind of helplessness, in the hit movie sequel *Superman II*, released in 1981, when the Son of Krypton chooses to surrender his otherworldly powers in order to feel more human, only to realize that he was meant to have them and that he can't be Superman without the Super. Lucky for him he could just ask for his powers back. Me, I had to get mine off the internet, from a place called Hot Hollywood Re-creations. You've got to do what you've got to do, I guess.

Instead of saying anything more, we both chose to gaze into the "Maui Sunset" and imagine that we were on the beach rather than trapped in a basement room with fiberglass insulation drifting down like fairy dust from the gaps in the ceiling tiles.

"I'm extending Lawrence's shift for a few hours and giving you the rest of the afternoon off," said Mr. Pastore, inking notes on his giant calendar. "He gets a ride home with Arnold, so he'd have to hang around the extra two hours, anyway. And I'd rather have him working the floor than smoking out back with that group of Satanists."

"They *do* tell good stories," I said.

"Well, he belongs on the floor," said Mr. Pastore.

"And where do I belong?" I asked.

He didn't answer.

MAGNET

WEDNESDAY AFTERNOON AT THE COFFEEHOUSE. SUMMER: WEEK TWO.
I sat with my legs up on a wrought-iron table that was hot
as a poker. The glare on my screen was too bright for work.
I was trying to turn some of my journal entries into poems.
But every time I tried to read, I squinted like I had glau-
coma. (In the last hour, my entire collection of screen-saver
photos had cycled through four times. That's how produc-
tive I'd been.)

It was about time for a refill.

Leaving my stuff, I slipped back inside. The guy at the
counter smiled at me and extended one arm. I handed him
my cup—fourth time's the charm. "Don't make me cut you

off," he said, trying to flirt.

I didn't even answer.

The Grind House was a small independent coffee shop in a strip mall in Arlington, Virginia. It didn't have a lot of customers. Ever. On the weekends it was the hangout for a team of cyclists who wore bright yellow gear. (It's a good thing the place wasn't into selling food. No one feels like eating around a bunch of skinny guys in spandex shorts.)

My brother, Faris, had introduced me to the place. When he showed me around, the first thing he did was point out the electrical outlets, knowing I'd need a power source for my laptop. Then he noted the items on the menu with clever names like "Magma Mocha." He knew I'd like that, too, or at the very least find it incredibly lame and irritating. Either way, he knew I would have an opinion. Lastly, he introduced me to Helen, the girl who worked the counter. She had a sweaty hippie vibe. She also had a habit of calling me "girl." But that wasn't why she annoyed me.

Helen was the real reason Faris liked the Grind House. She had a lower back tattoo. Her thong rode all the way up.

(Was it weird to be bitchy to a barista who was hot for your brother? I guess I didn't like it when Faris showed other girls attention. I was his baby sister. I was supposed to be the only apple of his eye, or something.)

That was a long time ago. I hadn't seen Helen in months. And despite finding the shop so annoying it practically made my eyes water, I came back. Almost daily. The Grind House had been anointed by my brother. It was sacred ground.

As I stood at the counter waiting, I paged through a book called *Take Back Your Life: A Guide to Grabbing Life's "Bull" by the Horns*. It was a self-help guide from the "Take a Book, Leave a Book" shelf at the front of the shop. It was total shit. But I needed all the help I could get.

"You want room for cream?" the kid asked.

"Nope," I said for the fourth time that morning. I liked my coffee black—like my hair, my nails, and my clothes.

Drink in hand, I headed back outside and sat down. Another customer had arrived, a big bald dude with a black mustache. He sat a few tables down with his dog, a boxer, reading the *Washington Post* real-estate section and taking notes on a pad of paper. I felt guilty. He was getting things done, and I wasn't. Waking up my computer, I stared at what I'd written. I hated it. Nothing I ever wrote sounded like how I imagined it in my head.

Had he needed me as much as I needed him?
Maybe more.
He was my hiding place,
but then he left,

46

became a closed door,
became a windowless room.
Love became an empty place, and all I heard
was my echo

Once we got lost in the city,
driving in circles without a road map.
"I didn't want to get anywhere anyway,"
he said

And as we stopped at one skeevy gas station after another
in all the wrong parts of town
all I could manage to do
was stare hypnotically at the double yellow lines,
the foreboding road signs.
"Do not pass" "Do not enter" "One way"
"Stop"

Why couldn't he understand?
I love boundaries.
They keep things in.
They keep things out.
They are there when you need them most

"Wow," said an excited voice, derailing my train of thought. "The Orient Espresso, what a great name for a drink."

When I heard that voice, my sensors beeped off the charts, and I glanced up. It was oddly familiar.

A few tables over, a young guy was kneeling down to admire the bald dude's boxer. The dog did that thing dogs do when they're so happy they could just die. Its eyes rolled back in their sockets, mouth hanging open.

"You're kidding," said the guy. "His name is Spike? That's like the name of every cartoon dog ever. It's like he might start talking, or get hit by a falling piano."

A mouthful of coffee trickled from my mouth as I realized how I knew him. I coughed into a napkin, flapping one hand uncontrollably as I tried not to choke to death. The guy was *him*. I. Could. Not. Believe. It. How in the hell did Sculpture Garden Guy, Folio entry number 108, "You're the most beautiful girl I have ever seen" kid, track me all the way out to Arlington, Virginia?

Leaning over, I dug around in my bag for my journal. I found it and slipped off the thick rubber band. This was the first time a freak had crossed state lines and found me. It was unprecedented. It was amazing.

It was a disaster.

Bringing my eyes up from the page, I gasped. He stood over me.

It was difficult to tell if he recognized me or not. If he did, there was no sign of it on his face.

"Hi," said the guy. Then he did the absolute worst thing

he could have done. He started to sit down in the chair across from me. "Is this seat free?"

"I'm sorry, my friend is sitting there," I hurriedly said. Then I pretended to get comfortable even though I'd been there for an hour.

He backed away from the table. "Which friend?" he asked.

"*My* friend."

His brow wrinkled. "You remember me, don't you?"

I broke eye contact—a sure sign of guilt—and looked down at the pages of my journal. It was almost like I was still facing him. Words described in detail the boy standing right in front of me. I was trapped. "No. I don't," I said as a bus passed, kicking a thick tail of smoke across the sidewalk. "People usually say, 'You don't remember me, do you?' not, 'You remember me, don't you?'"

"That would only be if I wasn't sure," he said, shrugging. "But you *do* remember me. I can tell."

I wasn't going to get out of this. He was too smart, too curious—too crazy. And we had a history, if such a thing was even possible.

"Fine, I remember you," I said. Then I closed the Freak Folio and slid it into the center of the table. I liked having it there. I could handle my version of this guy, no problem, but I wasn't letting the real McCoy anywhere near me.

"And you're not here with a friend," he said.

"No, I'm not, but I *am* busy."

49

"Why are you here alone?" he said, not budging. "You shouldn't be alone."

"I like being alone," I said, starting to grow exasperated. "So hint, hint, I can't be any clearer."

"No, you don't," he said, "like being alone, I mean. Introverts don't read self-help books that teach people skills and networking. CEOs aren't shy. Ask one."

"I was reading it as a joke, to be ironic," I said, which was only partially true. "Not everyone needs validation from strangers."

"Oh, I know that," he said. "You just look like someone who people would want to be around, so I was surprised to see you sitting by yourself."

Another random compliment. People were never this nice to me. Not my mother. Not my sister. Not anyone. "Thanks," I said cautiously.

Now that I saw him, I realized that I'd remembered him wrong. He was handsome, in a rugged, asymmetrical way. His bright blue eyes shook, like his skull could barely contain them. He carried himself with confidence. (Why did that surprise me?)

Stretching, he got back to his feet. "I don't want to keep you from the work, so I'm going to head back yonder from whence I came."

He circled the table to leave but then paused again. "Can I ask you a question?"

"If you're still planning to leave, you can do anything you like."

"That's fair," he said, nodding. "Um, so why do you hate me so much?"

As it was during our first meeting, his face held no trace of dishonesty. He leaned in expectantly for the answer.

"I don't hate you," I said truthfully. "I don't *know* you."

"Yeah, but you treat me like I did something horrible," he said, voice rising and accelerating. "Like I keyed your car, or kidnapped your baby and sold him on the black market, or something. I just saw you that once, and I said something nice."

"Sounds about right," I said, bristling a bit from the accusations. But at the same time he had a point. (Disregarding all of society's uptight "rules" of conduct, what exactly had he done wrong?)

He started fumbling over his words. "It's not nice to pass judgment on people you don't even know."

"I don't do that."

"You did it to me."

I wanted to be honest while still being understanding. "Well, everybody does it," I ended up saying.

"I don't."

This made me laugh. "Not everyone likes to be chased down by strangers. Seriously, dude. I always thought stalkers were supposed to stay hidden."

"I'm not a stalker," he said. It came out like he was a whiny kid. Balling his hands into fists, he jammed them down into his pockets. "I just wanted to say something nice because no one ever says anything nice." He glanced up. "Do you even remember what I told you?"

"I don't recall," I said, and was back to lying again. Against my better judgment, I had grown slightly interested in this guy. He was strangely well-dressed, with a white collared shirt and plaid pants that were either vintage hip or actual hand-me-downs from an old person. Also, it didn't hurt that he was good-looking, light hair and those light eyes, a strong jawline. The combined effect was that of a surfer dressed for court. More important than everything else, though, was that he was fascinating to talk to. It was the only predictable thing about him.

"Well, I *do* remember," he said. "I'd never done anything like that before."

"Really?" This came as a shock to me. "*You?*"

"Yes, I've chased down people to give them change they forgot at the cash register, and this one time I chased down a guy I thought had hit another person's car and fled the scene, but he was actually just slowing down to put a Chinese menu under the windshield wiper. But I've *never* chased down a girl before."

"It sounds like it was bound to happen sometime."

"Maybe," he said. "But I doubt it."

The conversation had ended, but we still gazed at each other. Not glaring or making eyes or any of that other crap. We just each looked at the other's face for a few extra seconds. I didn't know what had happened, but *something* had.

"What's your name?" he asked.

"I'm not telling you," I said.

"Okay," he said. "Mine's Charlie. Charlie Wyatt."

Then he was gone, and he hadn't even bought a coffee.

Half an hour later, I was parallel parking along Massachusetts Avenue. It wasn't easy. I kept thinking about Charlie Wyatt. This did not lend itself to concentration.

I was jarred from my meditation by a knock. A girl pressed her face against the passenger side window. She wore a shiny purple wig and an orange halter top that showed off her midriff. Her stomach was flat as a cake pan. Glitter speckled her cheeks. Knocking on the glass, the girl insistently mouthed two words. They looked to be *Real estate!* or *Worm Lame!*

That was my sister in a nutshell. Everything about her was either cute and sweet or inexplicably weird.

I leaned over, pumping the handle to roll down the window. (Yes, my car was one of those. I still had manual windows. Everything about me was work.)

"We're late," said Maggie. She leaned inside to unlatch the door. My sister was a girl of action. "You were supposed to be here ten minutes ago."

"And you were supposed to dress up," I said, cutting the engine.

"Like that was going to happen," said Maggie, collapsing into the passenger seat. "Status report: they were out of *Hulk*, but all is not lost, because I met a hot guy."

"Of course you did. What about Pill?" I was referring to Maggie's on-again, off-again summer romance: a lanky neohippie who wore a top hat and worked at a shop in Georgetown called Hellish Comics. (Every summer the two of them picked up their relationship where they'd left off the year before; they'd been doing this for five years.)

"Me and P are not serious," she said, getting comfortable, the butt of her vinyl shorts squawking against the upholstery.

Maggie always squeaked or squawked or squelched. This was because she was a cosplayer. Her hobby was dressing up like characters from Japanese cartoons and comic books. Thus vinyl made up a majority of her wardrobe. Today she was dressed as Kiki Dash. Kiki was a robotic bounty hunter with purple hair, boots, and the aforementioned midriff. Cosplayers were supposed to dress up for conventions and contests. My older sister liked to throw her own one-woman conventions. Like, daily.

One look at my face and she knew something was on my mind. She laid a hand on my arm. "You okay, Glory?"

"I'm conflicted," I answered, thinking about my mysterious admirer, who I now knew to be one Charlie Wyatt, coffee-shop patron. (It was always harder to forget freaks when I knew their names.)

"You wouldn't be *you* otherwise," she said with a wink. "Now come on."

We got out of the car and walked around to the back. I popped the trunk, and we stood there together staring into the payload. It was full of food—stuffed grape leaves, spinach pies, hummus—but most importantly, cookies.

Every month, our mother's "friends" held a get-together; and by "friends" I mean donors. They consisted mostly of fancy Lebanese women who met in an old brownstone near Embassy Row. That's the neighborhood where foreign diplomats lived in high-gated mansions. The venue said a lot about the partygoers. They had money, lots of it.

When it came to causes, my mother was an addict. Her day job was as an attorney prosecuting hate crimes. Once a week she hosted a radio show about public policy on NPR. She wrote freelance articles on international law for overseas newspapers. But the biggest responsibility in her life was her position as director of the Arab American Advocacy Council, a foundation she started before I was born.

(Notice how I didn't say her biggest responsibility was her family? Yeah. I noticed, too. So did my father. That's why he left when I was four years old. Case closed, as they might say around the law offices.)

Maggie and I were twenty minutes late when we finally wobbled into the house, trays in hand. Mom stood waiting for us, frowning.

Every time I saw my mother, it hit me: no lady has ever been so beautiful. Her small black dress was immaculate. Not a speck of lint. Her ears and throat gleamed with diamonds. Sometimes her perfection made her look like a toy, a doll. She was so put together, so well dressed, and so perfectly painted. It wasn't fair that someone who'd been through such hell could look so untouched by it.

The second she caught sight of Maggie in her purple hair and bounty-hunter cleavage, Mom's face went blank. "You cannot wear those clothes in here," she hissed. "This is someone's home."

"Like I've never met your friends," said Maggie with a smirk.

Mom clamped her jaw shut. "Well, at least button up. No one here wants to stare at your breasts all afternoon."

"I know, isn't it terrible?" said Maggie, hustling down the hall with her tray overhead, like a waiter. "I should find another party."

"And what about you?" Mom asked. She turned her penetrating gaze on me.

"What did *I* do?" I asked.

She couldn't think of anything, so in a whiny voice she said, "You're late."

"Sorry," I said, annoyed. "Not much I can do about traffic."

Mom glared at me. "These women contribute large sums of money to the foundation, and they must be well taken care of. Without them, I couldn't do a thing and the annual dinner would be out of the question."

I returned her cold gaze. "Maybe next time you should get someone more reliable to run your errands."

Our staring contest continued.

Suddenly there was a chorus of greetings from another room. "Margaret! It's so good to see you!" and "You're looking quite shiny today!" This meant that my sister had made her big entrance at the party. Mom immediately switched into damage-control mode. Yanking the two trays from my arms, she hurried down the hall toward the kitchen. Her heels clicked loudly as she went.

I watched her go. She belonged with them, the phonies. There wasn't a genuine thing about any of them. (And that wasn't even taking into account the plastic surgery.)

With a well-earned sigh, I wandered into the dining room. After years of fundraising and schmoozing, I knew this old house well. The hardwood floors gleamed. The antique coffee sets had been polished. Every one of the black-and-white family portraits had been dusted. I'd always liked those photos best. A hundred ancient faces hanging on the wall. They were immigrant families, wearing plain dresses and musty neckties. It was odd how shallow my mother and her friends seemed; especially with the humble relatives who came before. Some of their fathers had jumped off ships in Liberty Harbor and swum to shore in their soaked suit coats.

Exiting the front door, I stepped back outside into the dwindling heat of the afternoon. I sat on the stoop, legs down the front steps in the sun. I felt so alone. There was a huge world out there, but it all seemed miles away. I was just a voyeur.

A few minutes passed, and then I heard the door open behind me. Maggie dropped down next to me on the welcome mat. She leaned her head on my shoulder. A few pieces of glitter sloughed off and fell like snow to the steps below.

"What're you thinking about?"

"Where I can find an arsonist to burn this place to the ground," I said.

"Pill would probably do it; for cheap, too."

"I can't believe you still see that guy."

"He's easy to slip back into. Like a comfortable pair of sandals."

"Gross," I said.

She put a hand on my back, flat, strong. "Are you sure everything's okay?"

"Yeah."

"Liar."

"I miss Faris."

"Me too," she said. "He'd have had a field day with those bats in there."

Faris had been in Afghanistan only a few months when his APC hit a roadside bomb. He was twenty-one. That was nearing ancient for an active-duty marine corpsman. It was funny; he'd always seemed old to me. That's what big brothers are for, I guess. Faris had died a year ago, but nobody had quite gotten used to referring to him in the past tense. I wondered if we ever would.

I looked into Maggie's deep brown eyes. It was easy to imagine her without the lip gloss and shoulder holster. She was the same Maggie from my childhood; the same Maggie who covered me from the rain, even when there was only one umbrella between us.

Pulling her close, I ran my fingers through her purple hair. "Don't go back to college at the end of the summer, Kiki Dash," I said. "Stay. I'll wash your stretch pants. I'll groom your wigs."

She kissed me lightly on the cheek. "You don't need me," she said. "Anyway, I think I'm done with the dress-up; too many weirdos. I'm thinking about getting into online video games."

"Yeah, no weirdos there," I said.

I felt her eyes on me, but she didn't speak right away. "Did you ever show Mom any of those poems you wrote?" she asked at last.

"No," I said. "I only show you that stuff."

She rubbed my exposed arm. Her hands were still surprisingly cool in the heat. "Glory, you should let her read them," she said. "Your heart needs to breathe."

"Is that right?" I asked.

"Yes," she told me. "You've got it closed up in your chest, like you're holding it hostage."

"That's a good line," I said.

"I stole it," she said, smiling, "from one of your poems."

I couldn't help but smile back. I reached out and took her big hand. We both squeezed. Then I leaned into her, my head on her squeaky vinyl shoulder. And she held me.

That's what a big sister is for: to be there when your big brother can't be.

FREAK

THE SPRING IN MY STEP SAID IT ALL. I CHUGGED DOWN CLARENDON
Boulevard at a full sprint in my plaid pants and dress shoes,
backpack bouncing along behind me. I was still so excited
I could barely keep myself from tackling every jogger I saw
with glee. I flew right by them, and despite their best efforts
to keep up, they could only eat my dust. Every muscle tightened with excitement, and I almost gave myself a headache
clenching my jaw shut so hard.

Me. She talked to *me.*

If not for my chat with the beautiful girl from the Sculpture
Garden, it easily would have been one of the worst days in
a long while. Lucky for me, that encounter was like a snug

white life preserver. Despite the customer-service incident and subsequent talking-to at Family Friends, I no longer felt more than a gentle rolling of waves.

I hadn't felt this good in months, not since I got the letter.

Ah, the letter. It came on a Friday morning this spring, just as I was going in to check on my mom and help her to the bathroom for her morning pee. This was actually one of my favorite parts of the day—the coolness of the floor on my bare feet, the moon still white in the sky, the smell of the fresh coffee from the fancy coffeemaker we'd gotten as a Christmas gift from an uncle I'd never met who always incorrectly wrote my name as "Charley" as if I were an NFL cheerleader.

The letter had officially been delivered the day before but gotten wedged in between the pages of an L.L.Bean catalog, on the page advertising fishermen's waders. Right away I recognized the logo on the envelope: white satellite dishes aimed high into an indigo sky. It was the symbol for ALMA, or Atacama Large Millimeter Array. This ambitious research project would utilize an array of advanced radio telescopes to peer deep into the origins of stars and possibly into the genesis of our galaxy itself.

I'd entered an essay contest sponsored by the astronomy department of the University of California Santa Cruz, the winner of which would spend a month working on the ALMA site as it finished construction. There were thousands of contestants but there could be only one winner.

Me. They'd picked *me.*

But none of that mattered as I tore past a rotating sprinkler, getting the timing just right and staying dry all the way through. Chile seemed as far away as any distant planet. For the first time in a long time, I was glad to be right where I was.

I was so intensely focused on remembering the girl's every word, every glint in her big brown eyes, that I didn't notice when I turned left when I was supposed to have turned right. Stopping in the middle of the street, I took stock of the situation.

I get lost easily, and all the time. In order to read the street signs, I removed the bumpy crocodile skin case from my backpack and slipped on my huge, ugly glasses. The optometrist had ordered me to wear the glasses constantly because, according to him, my vision was deteriorating, and if his prognosis proved correct I'd be reading the *Annual Review of Astronomy and Astrophysics* in braille by the time I was thirty-five. That's what I get for spending most of my free time squinting through a lens the size of a dime.

I rubbed the ridges of the crocodile skin case against the creases of my palm. It had belonged to my mom. In it she'd kept her gold bifocals, which hung from a beaded chain that made a soft clacking whenever she set them on a table, like a rain stick. I still remember how she'd push them up her nose before reading, only to have them slip back down to the tip after a few seconds. She wore them every night to read me a bedtime story. I preferred comic books, and she enthusiastically obliged: voicing every caption box, every sound effect, and every villain's monologue. Now those same glasses sat virtually untouched on her nightstand.

Picturing my mom, I took a deep breath. Whenever I thought about what I'd be leaving behind, I questioned my decision to go away at all; and not just to South America this coming fall, but anywhere ever. Unlike most kids I'd met, my departure wasn't giving my parents an excuse to finally take that leisurely cruise around the Bahamas they'd always planned, complete with roulette night and a rock-climbing wall. No, when I left, I'd be turning my back on people who really needed me.

After a lot of hesitation, I put on the glasses and squinted through the thick lenses, and then, after walking in circles for a few blocks, I found the street name that I was looking for and headed home. I wasn't sprinting anymore; and from time to time I caught myself glancing at the sky, wondering when the stars would come out.

*　*　*

By the time I walked in the door of our tenth-floor apartment, it was five thirty: *Wheel of Fortune* time. I found Dad camped on the couch in his unbuttoned workman's shirt, watching the screaming faces of the contestants turning green and blurry in the upper right corner of the screen, where something had happened to the TV tube. The room lay dark. Sun peeked in from around the drawn shades, and particles of dust floated through the thin shafts of light.

Dad didn't notice me come in, because he wasn't expecting anyone. This was normally when he clocked out and left his office in the apartment building's basement to come back upstairs and drink a beer. He sat really deep in the cushion facing away from me, the balding circle at the top of his head like the white of an eyeball. A half-eaten sandwich sat on the coffee table next to a bowl of cheese-powdered curls. As always, he fanned himself with his Washington Redskins baseball cap; he'd never sprung for air-conditioning. "We already got it," he liked to say. "They're called sweat glands."

I don't remember the last time I'd seen my dad stationary. He was always on the move, zooming up and down the elevators to visit tenants, sliding under leaky sinks or into furnace room crawl spaces; even when he had his hands busy with something, he was also probably on his cell phone chatting to someone who needed him as soon as he was done with whatever it was he was currently doing. Dad was a fixer.

"Hi," I said, leaning on the doorjamb.

The TV turned off with a popping sound. "Hey," said Dad, whirling around. "There's my guy." A piece of avocado clung to his beard.

"You're home early," he said. "I didn't expect you for another hour."

"They let me off early."

Dad smiled. "Jerry isn't exactly a ball breaker, is he?"

I didn't answer but smiled, so he wouldn't worry.

"How are things over at the store?"

"Same old, same old," I said, eyes on the floor. The fabulous news of the girl in the coffee shop rose up in my throat, wanting to be heard, but now was not the time, and Dad was not the parent. I saved that sort of thing for my mother.

"What about you?" I asked. "Work okay?"

"Sure. Yeah. Work is work."

Dad was the superintendent of our building, Soleil Day Apartments, and he had been for about ten years. He lobbied hard for the position, wanting to work from home so he could always be in the same building as Mom. Plus it was the ideal job for him. The only thing that my dad seemed to understand more than heating, plumbing, and electrical systems was people. In fact, it's pretty incredible that he and I were related at all. When tenants saw him coming, their faces lit up; when they saw me inbound, they took off in the opposite direction.

Scratching his hairline, Dad grabbed the arms of the chair and pushed off to his feet. Then he walked over and pretended to stretch so he could be in the ideal position to slap a hand on my shoulder, which he had to reach up to do. I'd outgrown him in the last few years, not that anyone was really keeping track of that sort of thing.

"Who's responsible for dinner tonight?" asked Dad, smiling goofily. He pulled on the baseball cap and secured it in place.

"Actually," I said, "I think Edison is planning to come over and cook for us."

He beamed. "Paul's coming over? That's great news." Then he raised one finger and pretended to scold me. "Although I keep telling that boy to take you *out* of this apartment, not give you more reasons to stay in."

"How's Mom?" I asked.

"She's resting, having a fine day," he said. "I have the monitor on."

Hanging my backpack in the small front closet, I popped off my shoes and hurried down the hallway to see my mom; but I was interrupted by a knock at the door.

It was loud and rapid, and caught us both by surprise. Dad

jumped so dramatically that I expected him to hit his head on the hanging light fixture. No such luck, of course.

"Open up, Wyatts!" shouted a voice. "This is the United States Food and Drug Administration! We've come to confiscate whatever it is that's causing the smell in the vegetable drawer of your refrigerator!"

A wide grin spread across Dad's face. "Speak of the devil."

We found Edison sitting in the hallway, still wearing his gray driving gloves and expensive black sunglasses. He reeked of menthol cigarettes, one of his many vices. On his lap rested the flat black leather portfolio he carried with him everywhere, and an ordinary brown paper grocery bag with handles. Underneath his arms were two dark circles of sweat where he'd soaked through his shirt.

He smiled when he saw us and extended one hand. "Nice to see you again, Mr. Wyatt."

"You know better than that," said Dad, shaking my friend's muscular arm. "Only a few people can call me Jacob, so take advantage." Like he did every time Edison arrived, Dad crossed the room to the window and tugged open the Venetian blind so he could peer out over the crowded apartment parking lot. "My, my, my," he said, whistling. The metal blind pinged under a finger. "She's looking good."

"Dad," I said, "we're ten floors up. You can't see his stupid car."

Edison owned a vintage 1970s Chevy Nova that he'd equipped with hand controls, hydraulics, and neon ground effects. He also drove like a lunatic. It seemed to me that he was out to prove that the car accident that had paralyzed him at the age of thirteen wouldn't in any way keep him from paralyzing someone else. No, sir. He was a stupid teenage driver, just like the rest of us—well, except for me. I didn't have a license to operate a motor vehicle.

Sometimes it seemed like Edison's crash affected me more deeply than him . . . at least on a philosophical level. After it happened, I made it a priority to be with him. At the end of each school day I walked fifteen blocks to the Metro station, took the Orange Line into DC, and then caught the H2 bus to the Washington Hospital Center, where I sat with him at the table in his room and played the board game Settlers of Catan. That or I tried to make him see my side in our friendship-old Superman versus Batman argument. I saw him suffer. After those long nights, and the years of physical therapy that followed, I was in no hurry to get behind the wheel of a car. If Ray Bradbury didn't need a driver's license, neither did I. Edison, however, got his on the day he turned sixteen.

"You guys go ahead and hang out," said Dad, pushing Edison into the front hallway. "I'm going to see if your mom feels up to joining us."

"Sounds good," said Edison as he wheeled down the plastic runner into the dining room. Years ago, Dad had put down protective mats in most of the rooms so Edison's wheels wouldn't streak the carpet, as if it was nice. I'd seen bowling alley carpet that was more expensive. The living room was just as my mom had left it five years ago, not a cheap throw pillow out of place, the fuzzy purple sofa spotless and wrapped in a zipped-up plastic cover. Every painting was so level you could have set a marble on the frame and it wouldn't have rolled a millimeter in any direction.

I didn't even wait until we were alone before talking. "Guess who I saw today?"

"Who'd you see?"

"Guess." I took my hands out of my pockets. They wouldn't stop clenching and unclenching in fists, which always happened when I had to reveal information gradually so as to make it interesting to other people, anecdotal. That's how others seemed to like their information. Me, I could just talk, forever if they let me.

"I'm not guessing, dude. It takes me an hour to get ready for bed. Talk."

"That girl I saw downtown last week," I said, unable to hide the smile.

"Which girl?"

"The girl from the deli downtown. The one I chased."

It took a second, but then his jaw dropped, and then he pointed at me accusingly. "You are full of it," he said. "You are lying."

"Nope," I said.

"I wouldn't have guessed that in a trillion years," he murmured, scratching his chin. "Did you talk to her? What the hell did she say?"

I didn't want to go into detail, as Edison had a nasty habit of seeing the worst in everything, at least in what I told him. So I said, "She's coming around."

"Which means she told you to drop dead," he said.

"She said nothing of the sort," I told him. "Like I said, she's coming around. We're establishing what one might call 'a relationship.'"

"Does *she* know about this 'relationship'?" he asked.

"Maybe," I said.

Coasting across the clear plastic mat, he slapped me on the lower back. "You are officially the luckiest and unluckiest person I have ever met."

This didn't make sense. "Why am I both?" I asked.

"Because in your addled mind, you think that bumping into this girl is a good thing. But, brother, it couldn't be worse."

From the kitchen came a shout of "Soup's on!" This meant that Dad was hungry and wanted Edison to start making

71

him dinner. Not once had I heard that shout, walked into the kitchen, and actually found any soup "on" anything.

For the next thirty minutes, Dad and I stood around the kitchen watching like idiots as Edison whipped together a culinary masterpiece from groceries he'd brought with him in the brown paper bag. Most of the food we kept in the house was meant specifically for Mom, ingredients to pump up her calorie and protein intake and that would be easy for her to swallow. As for Dad and me, the continuous survival of the Wyatt men could be directly linked to the invention of the microwave oven.

When Edison finished, we sat down to a three-course meal of pasta with a cream sauce, Italian salad, and some kind of gooey chocolate glop for dessert. And we talked—about normal stuff, like how work was a pain in the butt no matter what you did for a job, and how we were already sick of all the hype about a movie in which reanimated dinosaurs fought robots from the future. Secretly, though, I was buying into the hype—*dinosaurs* fighting *robots*! Come on! No matter which side loses the war, it's the audience that wins. I didn't admit it, though, because I didn't want to be left out. I felt that way too often as it was.

During the conversation about work, Edison told us stories about his art internship at this big video game company. His stories were about drawing castles and monsters, or working with talented and creative people who were so interesting they couldn't ever get along. So far, my only good work story was about discovering rats in the ceiling tiles above the employee bathroom.

As we started drinking our after-dinner coffee, Edison left the room, and when he reappeared he was carrying his leather portfolio. "Check this out," he said. He opened the huge black case with a creak of its binding and laid it open faceup on the table.

"Holy cow," said Dad.

"Whoa," I muttered. Turning the pages, Edison revealed a world of gruesome monsters and weird, man-eating freaks that must have crept straight out of his warped mind. His twisted creations scattered across the pages like bugs running from the light. One guy had tentacles for legs, with hooks and suckers and everything. Another guy was made entirely of bones—not human bones but a collection of random animal skeletons, some that I didn't even recognize, and more that were probably imaginary.

They reminded me of creatures from the Bizarro World, also known as the planet Htrae, a fictional setting that was introduced in the Superman mythology of the 1960s. Everything in Bizarro World was recognizable but altered in some fundamental way, often the opposite of what it was on Earth. Ugly was beautiful. Failure was success. Normal people were monsters. As I was growing up, I often wished real life was the opposite of how it was—that sad was happy, or sick was healthy. When you put it that way, Bizarro World wasn't so bizarre after all.

"These are for computer games?" asked Dad.

"Online games," said Edison, grinning. He loved the compliments, the reactions. I couldn't help but wonder what it was like to have a talent that touched people in an unexplainable place, one that knocked the wind out of them. Both he and Dad had the ability to connect in a way I never could. For some reason, the average person doesn't seem to find the differences between elliptical, spiral, and irregular galaxies as arousing as I do. Go figure.

I pointed at one illustration in the sketchbook that didn't seem to fit with the others on the page. It depicted a tall, white-haired guy rippling with muscles, his chest stuck out and bearing the symbol of a dynamic blue *C*. I immediately liked the look of him.

"What's that?" I asked.

Edison didn't answer at first, and a shrewd little grin cracked at the corner of his mouth. "That's you," he said.

A few seconds passed and then we all started to laugh. Actually, we roared. It felt good in a way I can hardly describe, like remembering where you left something you've lost, and then finding it right at the very moment you need it most.

Of course, only Edison and I were really in on the joke. My dad had no idea I wore a prop Superman costume under my clothes every day.

He just thought I was your average high school junior who was convinced he'd discovered a comet.

By eight o'clock, Edison had gone, and Dad was off on a house call—someone's chandelier was on the fritz—so I slipped into Mom's bedroom, where she still lay sleeping on the bed like a speed bump in floral sheets. Only she was waking up, stirring with a groan and a tremor.

I gradually pulled up the light's dimmer switch and then shut the door behind me.

"Hi, Mom," I said slowly, cheerfully, and walked to her bedside, sitting in the chair near the headboard. I set the tray on the floor near my feet. It held a glass of water with a straw and a bowl of specially made cereal. Reaching over the safety bar that lined the edge of the mattress, I touched her wrist, gently, but enough to let her know I was there, in case she couldn't tell. "I'm here."

It took a few minutes. Then she spoke. At first, all she could manage was a sigh, but then out came a "Charlie," just for me.

Sometimes that was all she said. More and more words had evaporated during the last few months. I prayed that when

75

the time came, my name was the last thing she could ever say, that everything around her, everything on Earth, could be summed up simply as "Charlie." I think that would be a wonderful way to be remembered, in that soft voice.

I remembered my mom from when I was young, the sounds of her singing at the living room piano. She rarely took out the sheet music when she played and would sit for hours at a time without ever getting up once. You never knew when she'd play, or what. Something inside her would just click, and then she'd sit, brushing the bench's red velvet cushion with the flat of her hand, perching so delicately on one end of the hump like a woman riding sidesaddle. I could dream it so easily, without even needing to close my eyes. Before she'd start to sing, she'd say, "This one's for Charlie."

Remembering this made me smile.

"You've eaten a lot today," I said, picking up the bowl of cereal. "I don't know where you're stashing it, but I'm going to find out." Reaching behind her back, I helped her sit up against the pillows. Her pretty, pale face frowned back at me as if I hadn't said anything. That expression haunted me. Wisps of blond hair frizzed up from around her forehead, and she noticed me glancing at them and reached up with one clumsy arm to pat them down. Every day I spotted new wrinkles as her face caved in under the strain of sickness. Once, she had been Dad's youthful bride, two years his junior. Now she looked like she could be his mother.

There are some steadfast rules when communicating with someone with Huntington's disease. It takes a patient caregiver to see through all the semblances of madness to understand what is really going on inside a sick person's head. I know that I sometimes came off as a little awkward around other people, discombobulated, even frantic, but when I needed to, I could forget the world, just let it slow to a crawl around me as I waited, listening. "Are you hungry?" I asked.

"It's snowing," she answered. When speaking to a person with Huntington's disease, you should never pretend to understand what they are trying to tell you if you don't. Always ask them to try again. You have to keep trying until you get it.

"Are you hungry?"

"Yes, honey."

I held out a spoonful of cereal.

Mom took the handle of the spoon and then held it quivering for what seemed like a week. It was for that very reason that we had all the clocks removed from her bedroom. Time slowed to a crawl behind those dark curtains, which she insisted on having pulled shut for hours on end, day after day, despite the momentum of life outside.

A sudden spasm sent the spoon to the sheets, splattering the food.

MAGNET

I WOKE WITH A HEADACHE. OH, AND A DREADFUL FEELING OF TOTAL
and incomprehensible loneliness. Typical.

Sun soaked my yellow curtains. Through the fabric I
could see every twist of the tree branch outside my window. A garbage truck idled in front of a neighbor's house,
engine rumbling. When it finally pulled away with a series
of screeches and clunks, birds filled the emptiness with song.
I could still smell the stink of trash, though. It turned my
stomach.

It was going to be one of those days.

I sat up against the wall, head pounding, strangely sweaty.
Goose bumps covered my skin. I took a deep breath and

rubbed my arms for warmth. Didn't feel cold, really, which was a little weird. Chills and nausea weren't usually associated with eleven hours of uninterrupted sleep. (Laziness, perhaps, but not so much the queasiness.)

A dark skid of black mascara marked the sheets where I'd been curled up asleep. Burrowing my feet under the comforter, I accidentally dislodged a stack of books that sat on the chest at the foot of my bed. It avalanched to the floorboards with a series of loud thuds. The topmost book fell open, as if on cue.

If anyone had walked in right then, I'd have died from embarrassment. A squished and worn library copy of *The Joy of Sex*, one that I'd stolen—yes, stolen—lay cracked at the binding, face open. It showed unspeakable things. (Sure, they were things that I'd done, but that doesn't necessarily make me proud of them.)

I snatched *The Joy of Sex* off the carpet and put it back where it belonged: behind the computer manuals and spare ink cartridges in my bottom desk drawer. Crossing the room was an obstacle course. I stepped over blank canvases, plates crusty with forgotten food, an electronic keyboard I'd bought used, back when I was convinced I wanted to be a songwriter (like Norah Jones, except without any talent). Nothing seemed to hold my attention long enough for me to finish it. Even the plants on the windowsill had long dried up.

I glanced down at the book's cover one last time and slipped it back into the drawer. There it could do no harm. The title was pretty misleading. I'd had sex a few times. Joy never had much to do with it. Adults build up sex into the experience of a lifetime. But your bed always ends up empty again. You always end up empty, too. Besides, after Faris died, I just didn't see any reason to seek intimacy in that way, or in any other. (Loneliness worked just fine for me, thank you very much.)

I straightened up, peering out my window into a street that was coming alive very slowly. Then up at the smoky gray slate roofs of the homes across the street. Sunlight winked at me through the leaves. I raised a hand to my eyes, squinted. That wasn't just the break of dawn winking. Oh no, I knew better than that.

"Good morning, Peter!" I called with a wave.

Peter Hopper or, as I like to call him, "the reason I started wearing a bathrobe," was just a little kid, probably ten. He was the son of a world-famous philanthropist and a former state senator. He was also a Peeping Tom.

I had blinds, so I used them. I had pajamas, so I wore them. They were Maggie's hand-me-downs and featured Wonder Woman. Peter could ogle *her* all he wanted.

The Freak Folio stared up at me from where it rested on my desk. It sat beside a framed picture of me and Faris posing together in front of the reflecting pool on the National

Mall. That photo looked more ancient every day. Might as well have been hieroglyphs.

Peter Hopper was the reason I'd started my Freak Folio in the first place. He was there, peeping at me, on the wrong morning. Call it fate. Call it whatever. I was sick of feeling vulnerable.

I'd always kept a journal, but it was only after Faris's death that it became an obsession. I felt safer writing about the freaks wandering the streets. It made me feel like less of one. So one day I started writing, cataloging. The rest, as they say, is history.

Now, spotting Peter Hopper was routine. By recording the pint-size pervert in my Freak Folio, I was turning the tables on his little nudity stakeout. I tugged off the fat rubber band and skimmed the pages of the journal.

That's when I found this:

Where would the talk between us have gone
had he stayed
had we sat facing each other
clutching our coffees but not our tongues?
Perhaps we could have pounded it out.
It wasn't attention. No it was his mother's love
or a childhood dream unfulfilled.
And maybe he could have fixed me, too.
Or at least told me how I was broken.

And there, staring back at me, was a sketch I'd made of Charlie Wyatt.

"Yikes," I said out loud.

I forgot all about being ogled and sat gazing at the picture. I hardly remembered drawing it. It made me sad. First of all, it was awful, and I was secretly relieved that no one else could see it. More important, though, was that I'd drawn him as a monster. But he'd never done anything to me, really. Except be nice, even patient, which was obviously hard for him. Why was I so hung up on Charlie Wyatt?

Sometimes I hated my Freak Folio. It showed me the pettiness I was capable of. I knew drawing that sketch was just an extension of my own anger, of how I saw the world. Still, I was ashamed.

Instead of closing the book, I picked up a chunk of graphite from the desk. And I began to draw. As I did, I fished a crumpled pack of cigarettes out of a desk drawer.

I finished Charlie Wyatt, the right way. I softened the edges and unbugged his crazy eyes. I remembered him how he really was and not how I'd made him. I worked until I was satisfied I'd done him right. He deserved that much for telling me I was beautiful, especially when I hadn't felt that way in ages.

I stuck a bent cigarette in my mouth and went about prepping a match. I didn't smoke. Not really. It was an occasional release. And a gross one.

Just then I knew someone was at the door, and I was up before the knuckles had even finished knocking. This was a skill I'd perfected over months of having a boyfriend secretly sleep over. Sure, it was a long time ago, like, sophomore year, but some habits die hard. The cigarette vanished out the window (like the boyfriend often did).

"Gloria?"

"Uh-huh?"

"Are you in there?"

"No, I'm throwing my voice from the kitchen. Can I get you anything?"

"Very funny." Pause. "Are you smoking in there?"

"I don't smoke, Mom." Pause. "Come in."

My mother opened the door but did *not* come in. She rarely progressed farther than the hall carpet. As if I'd splashed my doorway with sheep's blood and she were the Spirit of Death. I knew she had her suspicions about what I did in my bedroom. They were enough to ward her off. As with everything with her family, she could avoid dealing with it if she pretended it didn't exist. The system worked. Everybody got what they wanted.

"I can't believe you live like this," she said, craning her neck to see around inside my bedroom.

"Like what?"

"So cluttered and confusing," she said. "You live messily, my darling."

"I live *interestingly*."

She harrumphed. "Well, I won't argue with that." She still wore her silk bathrobe embroidered with Chinese calligraphy, shiny black hair swept up into a pair of gold pins. She was always elegant, gorgeous right out of the sack. Not like me. Not messy. Not cluttered, or confusing.

"You should get out and see your friends," she said. "Or invite them over. It would give you a good excuse to tidy up."

"I don't have any friends," I said. "Besides, who has time for friends with all this tidying to do?"

"Are you feeling okay?" she asked, hovering over me.

"Always," I said, shifting positions, "never better." I couldn't get comfortable, no matter how I tried.

"You look white," she said softly.

"White like a mime? Or white like George Bush?"

"The sick kind."

"So both?"

"I don't understand," she said.

"It's just nerves or something," I said, hinting that she'd worn out her welcome. She was right, though. I didn't feel well.

"You should eat the leftovers from your Chinese takeout. It's just sitting in the refrigerator waiting for you girls *not* to finish it." She shook her head. "What a waste."

The night before, Maggie and I had crashed on the couch

in front of the TV. One of the pay-cable channels was showing an erotic horror film marathon (yes, those do exist). Maggie was into the erotic stuff. And me, I just liked watching stupid people get what's coming to them. We could barely see the screen over the Great Wall of Chinese food that stretched the length of the coffee table in white cardboard cubes. The food didn't sit well. But since when have visceral gore and teriyaki beef ever made for an appetizing combination?

"Sounds, um, delicious. . . . So, are you leaving?" I said, hoping to change the subject from my eating habits back to whatever she'd come to say.

"Maggie and I are going shopping," she answered. "She needs something nice for the foundation dinner. You haven't forgotten about it, have you?"

"That'll be fun," I said flatly, dodging the question. Mom was going to force my sister into browsing ordinary things, like blouses or clogs. Only her plan would backfire when Maggie wound up shopping for a rubber bustier or aviator goggles.

My mother paused, thought. "Want to come with us?"

I wanted her to leave, to go do what she did and get on with life. Shaking my head, I got up. To stand was hell. "No."

"Well, you'll need to get something to wear eventually," she said. "I'll be on my cell, if you need me."

"I'll be fine," I said, getting tired of the effort it took to have a conversation with her. Then I added, icily, "I'm sure you'll be fine, too. You always are."

She didn't say good-bye. Palms pressed to my forehead, I watched her descend the hallway stairs, tall, poised, and forever unfazed. She didn't need some crazy guy telling her she was beautiful. I'm sure it happened to her all the time. (If only I could have borrowed some of her cup size, and maybe some of her class. In return I would have loaned her my sense of humor.)

Once she was gone, I walked to the bathroom to freshen up. I had me a date with some extra-strength Tylenol. But when I reached the door, I found it locked. I heard a soft crying on the other side.

"Hello?" I whispered, scraping my nails on the wood.

"Glory?"

"No, it's the Green Lantern," I said. "You okay in there?"

With a squeal, the door inched open to reveal my older sister hunched over the toilet, mid vomit. I could see that she'd been interrupted in the middle of taking a pee, as her cargo pants were still bunched around her ankles, leaving her naked from the waist down. I dropped to one knee to help. There wasn't much I could do.

"Don't tell Mom," she said before anything else.

"Right," I said, trying hard not to laugh.

"Pill," she said, staring up at me with eyes full of fear.

"What kind?" I asked, standing up and opening the medicine cabinet.

"No . . . *Pill*," she said. She meant her on-again, off-again summer fling.

"What about him?" I asked.

"Do you think he'd make a good dad?"

I didn't understand.

One more look was all it took to give her away. You can stuff a journal under a mattress or keep a sex book jammed in your bottom drawer. But nothing reveals the truth like a face full of terror.

"Oh," I said, getting it. And I always thought I was the quick one.

Yes, I eat as I drive. It's stupid, sure, but it's better than texting. Chinese is especially easy when you're skilled with chopsticks—one hand working the wood, the other working the wheel. No problem. I was doing my family a double service: acquiring sensitive items for my barfing sister, and making room in the fridge. Who says I'm useless? Oh, wait. I do.

I was having trouble getting my head around Maggie's potential impregnation. How could she have been so careless? Despite her peculiar interests (comic books and video games) and questionable wardrobe (leather chaps), she was surprisingly responsible, even . . . *conservative*. Wild girls get knocked up in college. Not girls with a 4.0. Not girls with full-ride chemistry scholarships. Not girls who left school for three months to move home and take care of their baby sisters after family tragedies. Those girls knew better.

Holding a box of kung pao beef in one hand, the wheel in the other, I pulled into the pharmacy parking lot. I opened the door to step out, nearly forgetting to put the car in park. It rolled a few feet before I wised up. Focus, I told myself. Focus. I had to be there for Maggie like she'd been there for me countless times before.

Head down, I bolted across the sidewalk and through the sliding doors into the air-conditioning. The place smelled like a counter that had seen one too many Handi Wipes. I didn't want to be there. Not one iota.

After scanning the big red signs, I made a beeline for the Family Needs section. There I found a wall of narrow little boxes. An army of expectant mothers glared down at me from the packaging with reproach.

(How, exactly, does one shop for a pregnancy test?)

Two teenage girls stood browsing the nearby condom rack. They were younger than me. Or *seemed* younger than me—the kind of girls who actually might end up pregnant and screw up everything they'd worked for, if they'd ever worked for anything.

"So how was it?" one asked.

"God," the other said.

"That bad?"

"England *sucked*."

"So sorry."

"I mean, my host family was *crap*."

I wanted to tell them to get lost so I could choose my sister's pregnancy test in peace. But I couldn't. Instead, I waited at the end of the aisle, pretending to compare the selection of designer footbaths. Finally they made a decision and turned toward the front of the store.

As they passed, one of them said in my general direction, "Sucks to be you." I couldn't tell which one spoke, since the girls were pretty much interchangeable.

It should never suck to be me; and then I thought about Maggie. I didn't want it to suck to be her, either.

"Hey."

I blinked. I'd started crying. A drop hit the pharmacy floor. I hastily wiped at my eyes, an instinct I'd developed over the past year of tears.

"Hey!" called the voice again.

At the end of the aisle, price gun in hand, stood Charlie Wyatt in a red vest. Oh. My. God. He worked there.

"Hey," he said again, quieter this time. No one wants to be

seen shouting at a girl across a pharmacy—especially if she's in the Family Needs section.

Acknowledging his general existence, I raised a hand and waved. I hoped to get by with just being recognized. That way he might only say hello without needing to take it any further. Of course, this was Charlie I was talking about.

As if to prove my point, he walked right up to me and said, "You look horrible."

"Jesus. Thanks a lot," I said. But he was right. I *felt* horrible. Every part of me was tingly and tired. Conditions clearly hadn't improved since my morning headache. Weird.

"I was thinking about you today," he said.

"Is that right?" I asked.

"I wondered what you took in your coffee, because of that time we bumped into each other at the Grind House."

"Fascinating," I said. "Don't tell me you're getting a job at the coffee shop, too. Then I'd have to change my whole routine." I was acting overly snarky because I was nervous; we stood in front of body lubricants and douche.

"No," he said. "I was thinking to myself, 'If I knew what that girl's name was, and where she was right now, I'd bring her coffee, just for the heck of it.' Of course, I only had three bucks on me, so I couldn't have afforded it anyway."

It was such a nice thing to say. It caught me totally off guard.

I examined Charlie Wyatt. Unlike every other boy I'd ever met, he didn't slouch. And he looked right into your face, right into your eyes. The gaze was so intense, I found myself looking away again, shaken. Even though his name tag didn't have fancy stickers or gold stars on it like another employee I'd seen, he wore his red drugstore vest with something resembling pride. Me, I would have been mortified.

"My name's Gloria," I told him. "Gloria Aboud."

Rubbing his chin, he stared distractedly at a bottle of massage oil. "I didn't think of that one," he said.

"What do you mean?"

"Well, I figured you for a Susie, a Nell, or a Madeline."

I squinted at him. "You're kidding, right?"

"No," he said. "My mom has an old baby name book at home, and I tried to decipher your name by using what I could assume might be your basic character traits, working backward and reading the descriptions first, then matching those to the names, if that makes sense." He paused. "It was really hard because"—and he laughed—"I don't, like, know you *at all*."

Instead of finding this incredibly creepy, which I probably should have, I found it endearing, because it was. "Don't you think Madeline is kind of a stretch?" I asked.

"Well, it was sort of the dark horse," he answered, shrugging.

He smiled at me. Thank god I stopped myself before I smiled back. That would have just encouraged him. I mean, what was I doing? I didn't have time for small talk, and besides, I detested small talk and all its implications. Didn't I?

"Listen, Charlie, I have to go," I said, feeling a sudden nausea.

Bad move. His eyes grew huge. "You remembered my name?" he asked.

How could I forget? Up to our encounter in Aisle Five, "Charlie Wyatt" was on the list of things I hoped to avoid. Like "traffic," or "herpes." Still, as much as I tried to avoid him, it seemed I couldn't. As much as I tried to forget him, I couldn't do that, either. (How do you wipe away the most annoying person you've ever met? Or the person who said the nicest thing about you that anyone's ever said?) "Name tag," I said, pointing to his.

He gave me a look that told me he knew I was lying and then said, "I can help you find something. That's what I do. I help people." He acted as though I wasn't doubled over, arms around my middle. My shirt stuck sweaty to my back.

I was experiencing a strong urge to go to the bathroom. And I didn't know why. I wasn't the one experiencing morning sickness. I hadn't even kissed a guy in, like, a year. So it was nada on the fertilized egg theory. But then how come I felt so . . . *ugh*?

"I think I can find what I'm looking for, thanks," I said.

"That depends on what you're looking for, because some of the new rainbow lawn chairs are still sitting in back on the delivery palette, so you can't really find them if they're what you're looking for." He edged in close to me, and he had a "clean" smell, barely even there. "But just between you and me," he whispered, "only three of those five chairs can be put out on the sales floor, because, well, I sort of wanted to see if they could hold my weight, so I stood on one of them, and then I started jumping on it, and it broke. So I had to test another to see if the first one was just a fluke. Well . . . it wasn't."

I registered only about half of whatever it was he was talking about.

"Hey, are you okay?" he asked suddenly.

Before I could do or say anything else, I started sinking slowly to the floor.

"I'm fine," I said at exactly the same time as my knees gave out. Gazing up, I lost myself in the dazzling fluorescents.

Charlie caught me with one arm. That was all it took. This struck me as my downward momentum came to a jarring halt. (He was stronger than he looked. He held me as if I were nothing more than a bird on his finger.) Reaching out, Charlie pulled a small stepladder away from the shelf and placed it gently behind me. I sat. Cramps twisted in the pit of my stomach.

Charlie was antsy. "We're not supposed to sit on the step-ladders," he whispered, "but I'm going to let you do it because you're a customer. Just make sure you end up buying something, all right?"

"Okay," I whispered back. My cheeks were hot. My feet were heavy.

"Tell me what's wrong," he said.

"Nothing," I said. "I just have to get one." And, stupidly, I gestured to the shelf.

He looked up at the ads and the packaging. "Pregnancy tests?" he said.

He was planning to say something else. Then the words melted on his tongue. "Oh," he whispered a few seconds later. "Oh, wow."

"No . . . wait," I said.

Again, he crept in way too close for comfort. "So, um, are you, like, going into labor or something?" he asked.

I pushed him away forcefully. "No! Jesus Christ, Charlie. It's not for me. I'm just feeling sick."

"Yeah, okay, I guess that makes more sense," he mumbled, looking a little confused, which was understandable, considering I was being confusing.

I started crying for no reason, wiping my face with a snotty sleeve. In my delirium, everything seemed worse, dire. Maggie would have a baby. Her life would be over (and Pill, with his nasty hair, would be my brother-in-law). My mother would kick them out of the house. Maggie would become a crack addict, turning tricks in between hits.

And Faris would still be dead.

And I'd still be alone.

"Talk to me," I told Charlie. "Make me feel better."

"Shouldn't I get somebody?" he asked.

"Talk to me."

"Talk about what?"

"I don't know," I said woozily. "Do you like working at a drugstore?"

"I get by," he continued. "It has its perks."

I wasn't sure if he meant his job at the drugstore or something else. "Like what?"

"The roof has a good view."

"What else?"

He shrugged. "Yesterday I found this big bag of discontinued Valentine's candies."

"Thrilling," I said.

His gaze drifted away from my face. It was so strange. I could practically feel his grip on me loosen as his mind wandered. "No, not thrilling, really, but interesting. See, the candies were a couple years old and were discontinued because the sayings on the tiny hearts were pretty weird, but I thought they were great." He stopped, probably letting his mouth catch up with his brain. "People are so used to valentines being sweet, you know, but these had an edge, saying stuff you might say to someone, like, after you pounded a couple beers and cut their heads out of pictures or something. Maybe you and this other person had a really long and checkered past, and this wasn't the first heart you'd given them, but the third or fourth in a series. And maybe the last."

I tried to imagine what he meant. It made me think of when I was younger, when we celebrated Valentine's Day at school. Everyone in class brought in a decorated box. Then we walked around the room filling each other's boxes with cards. There was always one kid who never got any. You always knew who it was going to be ahead of time. Every year, I'd wanted to slip a valentine into that person's little box, but I never mustered the courage to do it. Not with the rest of the class watching.

Charlie smiled, as if he'd forgotten where we were, what we were doing. "They reminded me of clues. You can't know the whole conversation, just this tiny slice of it, like a broken piece off a bigger whole. You have to take it at face value without knowing its role in some greater drama. That's what candy hearts are, really. You know, like clues. Like stars in a constellation."

I didn't know. But the way he put it, well . . . it was sort of pretty.

"Tell me one," I said.

He took a breath. "There's a lime green one that says, *I remember that time.*"

It gave me chills. Or maybe that was just the swoon.

"A yellow one says, *Did you mean it?* It tasted like dishwasher detergent."

"Those are amazing," I said.

"Want to know my favorite?"

"Sure," I said. It was weird. He could have recited candy hearts to me all day.

"*I'm torn,*" he said. The words settled in the silence that followed.

Charlie. He was a total weirdo. And he was a poet.

Every day I felt so much. I tried to write it all down, to make sense of it. But those feelings usually wound up hidden away in a book sealed with a fat pink rubber band. I didn't have the courage to share them with anyone. I didn't know anything about Charlie, other than what he'd told me. But I'd seen that a bunch of candy hearts nearly moved him to tears. And that says a lot.

Another wave of nausea hit me, hard, and I belched.

"Should I call a doctor?" he asked. I suddenly realized that he'd stopped talking a while ago. We'd spent the last minute looking at each other.

"No," I said. "Just get a bucket."

FREAK

"THIS ISN'T WORKING," I SAID.

I reached down and adjusted the driver's seat again, pushing it as far back on the track as it could go, and then tried to force it a few extra inches, which made a grinding metal-on-metal noise that I would have found annoying had I not been so focused on finding just that tad bit of extra legroom. The seat didn't budge. How is a person expected to drive someone else's car without making the proper modifications? Especially when he doesn't know how to drive.

"Charlie! It won't go back any farther."

"Well, I can't drive like this. This isn't a clown car. If it were, I'd be a clown. Do I look like a clown to you?"

Gloria sighed and slumped against the door. "It doesn't even matter. My house is just around the corner."

"Fine," I said, locking the sliding track into place, knowing I'd try again in a few seconds when she wasn't paying attention. "I'm done."

"Thank you!"

"You're welcome," I said. I pretended to doff an imaginary hat and then almost rear-ended a pickup truck with an American flag painted on the back window.

"Watch it, asshole!" the driver shouted, brake lights flashing.

"My bad," I said with a wave.

She closed her eyes. "I'm beginning to think this wasn't the best idea."

"Don't be ridiculous," I said. If I could have reached over and squeezed her hand to show her that everything was going to be all right, I would have, because you have to believe that—otherwise your whole life can spiral out of control and become one big "I'm beginning to think that wasn't the best idea." You have to draw the line. Everything can look like a bad idea if you choose to see it that way.

Gloria was not pregnant. I was glad. She gave me the whole story during a whirlwind trip to the Family Friends restroom, where she threw up about a gallon of Chinese food. My guess was food poisoning. It was against the rules for her to use the facilities, seeing as it was the employee restroom and she was not on the store staff, but I couldn't have cared less. I doubted Mr. Pastore would have wanted General Tso's chicken and kung pao beef spread across the display of beach toys. That would just be wrong.

"Watch where you're driving!" she yelled. "This is *my* car, remember?"

Gloria. I'd never seen a girl look so attractive while holding a bag of frozen peas against her forehead.

Driving her home through the summer rain had been her idea. She had prefaced it by saying, "I may be crazy but," a phrase that I was pretty used to.

I did not have a car, so I drove Gloria's, a midget Toyota with a coat hanger holding on the back bumper. The car was not at all what I had expected. The inside was wallpapered with stickers for rock bands I'd never heard of, like Brush with Death, and Human Stew, and Mega Dyke. A pile of battered CD cases slid around on the floor, disappearing under the seats every time you made a sharp turn. The back cushions were a landfill of empty coffee cups, discarded clothing, and old high school textbooks. Despite her presence beside me, I had trouble picturing Gloria behind the wheel—driving, brooding, and tossing trash over her shoulder as she screamed along with Mega Dyke.

"Hey! Four-way stop, idiot!" shouted a voice.

I turned sharply to avoid colliding with a minivan. "You're so right!" I called out my window to the other driver, waving.

"I'm going to die," murmured Gloria. "I am going to die a block from my house."

She clutched her head between her hands like it was a bomb and she had no place to get rid of it. Eyes screwed shut, lips taut, arms trembling, she looked sick, sure, but if anyone could make nausea look good, it was Gloria. I wasn't a doctor or anything, but when I was thirteen I'd gotten a parasite from eating a rotten crab apple. I remembered the symptoms, and occasionally still had flashbacks (in them, the crab apple eats me), and if I wasn't mistaken, the shuddering and sweaty lump of a person in the passenger seat of Gloria's Toyota looked awfully familiar.

I had to get Gloria home safe. That was my job. Everything else was unimportant, even highway safety.

"Over there," she said, pointing, head sliding lower down in the seat, "the red brick one."

"Affirmative." I guided the car along a curb of well-trimmed hedges with purple flowers blooming in the branches and into the long driveway. Stopping, I shifted gears down into park. I sat for a few seconds in the shade of the big brick manor, the grumble of the engine making the small snow globes on the dashboard shiver.

"That's your house?" I asked.

Now, I don't normally believe in signs. My philosophy is that if you start looking for signs, then you see them everywhere and in everything. That can be dangerous. Divination is not part of an astronomer's thought process or his goal when it comes to interpreting celestial systems. That's called astrology, and that's the same thing as superstition, with black cats, stepping on cracks, and all that.

Still, there had been times when I'd questioned my faith in the sciences.

For example, a couple years back I'd become enamored with a pretty young lady who worked at the local library. One afternoon after checking out, I found that a few of my books had been mistakenly switched with someone else's. Instead of a hardbound special edition of *Justice Legion*, I found a copy of *The Joy of Sex* in the bottom of my canvas bag. I took that as a sign—albeit a risqué one—that the girl had feelings for me, strong feelings. But when I confronted her with my suspicions, she rewarded me with a smack in the face. I lost a crown, and my pride, and my library privileges.

That was one example. Gloria's house was another.

"I used to mow your lawn," I said.

"What did you say?" she asked, hand on the door latch.

"Your grass—I cut it," I said.

She settled back into her seat. "We have a gardener,

Charlie." Then she squinted at me with those bloodshot eyes, as she tended to do. "You're not our gardener, are you?"

"Every Sunday afternoon," I said, opening the car door. "What are the odds?"

"Charlie, I've never seen you before last week," she said, and then with a shake of her head, she opened the door and lurched onto the driveway.

"When I was twelve," I clarified. "I mowed this lawn on weekends."

"Oh," she said, shaking her head.

I sat quietly, staring across the trimmed green lawn. When I was younger, I used to daydream about living in one of the mansions in her neighborhood but had to settle for spreading their mulch, bagging their lawn trimmings. My family rented an apartment, which was okay, I guess.

Apartments were pretty cool. They had balconies, with views where you could see the whole city or, in my case, where you could look down over bumper-to-bumper grid-lock on the Baltimore–Washington Expressway. Sure, one of our cats had leaped to his doom from the balcony railing, but I tried not to take that as some sort of commentary on his life with us. To be honest, though, after years on the tenth floor, I couldn't bear to live back down on the ground. The telescope in my bedroom window was that much closer to the sky.

I was so lost in thought that when Gloria stuck her head back into the car, it nearly gave me a heart attack.

"Keys, please," she said.

"Sure," I said, handing over the jangling mess. I got out of the car and closed the driver's side door. "So, you need some help inside?"

"Nope, I got it." But she didn't move and stayed slumped against the Toyota.

"Are you sure?"

Gloria slouched like her spine was a Slinky. "You're not going to go away, are you?" she asked. "Not unless I barf on you?"

"Probably not even then," I said honestly.

Sighing, she drummed her fingers on the car roof. "Fine, maybe you can come in and have something to drink. My family should be home soon."

"Thanks," I said, and then added, "I'm not crazy, just so you know."

She looked at me from under droopy eyelids. "If you weren't crazy, you wouldn't be here," she said. Then we walked up the path to the house. I gave her my elbow for support, and she took it without saying a word.

Once inside, I tried to do what was expected of a polite guest and I made myself at home in her perfectly arranged living room. Freshly cut flowers sprang out from a vase on the entryway table, giving the whole place a bright, lived-in appeal. A giant leather sofa with puffy armrests that reminded me of croissants hugged the maroon-painted wall. Above it hung an enormous black-and-white photo of a falcon, mounted lovingly between electric candle sconces, as if it were a masterpiece on display in a museum. Everything was dusted; everything was cleaned. Even the cushion covers had been ironed to leave thin creases in the suede. It was apparent that someone cared for this room. It took constant maintenance and a whole lot of love. Or money.

We had a few nice things once—so long ago I hardly remembered—but with Mom not working for the past five years we'd had to get rid of most of them. Dad had picked up our fuzzy purple sofa off the curb outside a frat house in Georgetown at the end of the spring semester, and we found our TV at a garage sale a decade ago, and it was so clunky we needed to borrow a wheelbarrow to carry it the eighteen blocks home. Most of the rest of what we owned was given to us by Soleil Day tenants wanting to help Dad out after all he'd done for them over the years. From what I could see, Gloria didn't even have a TV in her house. You know people are really wealthy when they actually choose not to have a television.

"I like your house," I called out.

"Thanks. Word on the street is that some weird kid used

to mow the lawn," shouted Gloria from down the hall. I heard a door close with a thump and then a toilet flushing. "We've only been here about five years."

"I remember coming inside," I said, "when the owners showed me around. They were friends of my mom's, the Andersons, I think. They showed me the whole place."

"Really?" she asked. "I don't know if I ever met them."

I closed my eyes and imagined walking through every room, just to see if I could remember them, and as I did, I couldn't help but wonder what this strange coincidence might reveal to me about Gloria. Did having spent time in her house give me special insight into who she was?

She came back into the room with a bottle of water in each hand. Collapsing on the opposite couch, she kicked her sandals onto the carpet and then downed an entire bottle in one gulp, making *glug-glug* noises. She tossed the other to me. Sweat still glistened on her forehead as she curled into her chair like a cat.

"Your house is much nicer than ours," I blurted out. "I think it's because you're cleaner than we are. Do you have a maid or something? Do you believe in hiring illegal immigrants as domestic help? Because I'm okay if you do."

Gloria stared as a drop of water trickled down one side of her mouth. "A cleaning service comes every two weeks."

"Are you rich?" I asked.

"No, we're not rich."

"What's your dad do?"

"Not applicable."

"Your mom?"

"She's an attorney."

"You're rich then, but that's okay—it's nothing to feel awkward about."

I couldn't read the expression on her face, which wasn't a frown but wasn't a smile, either. I sipped my water, and when I found it too warm to drink, I chose not to mention it.

"That's a pretty rude thing to say, Charlie," she said at last.

"Why is it rude?" I asked. "We both know it's true, so why pretend it's not?"

"Wealth is *how* you live," she said.

I thought about this, and it didn't make the slightest bit of sense. "No," I said, "wealth is how much money you have. *Happiness* is *how* you live. Listen, compared to the rest of the world, you are filthy stinking rich, but I am, too, and I sleep on a mattress we got from a frat house. What's the point in arguing over details?"

She stared some more, and then said, "Why are you so weird?"

"I seem pretty normal to me," I said.

"Well, you're not," she said, and then chuckled to herself. I didn't get the joke.

"Are you feeling better?" I asked.

"Much. Thanks." She eyed me cautiously.

She confused me. I really wanted to know what was going on in her head. I could have just assumed what she was thinking, like I did with everyone, but that didn't seem right. With Gloria, I didn't want to guess. I wanted to know, and that sort of scared me.

"Let's play a game," I said, "to take your mind off wanting to barf."

"Well, I'd forgotten about it," she said, sighing, "until now." She stood up. "I'm going to bed, Charlie."

"You want me to leave?" I asked. "Then who would you have to talk to?"

She thought about this. "What kind of game?"

"It's not so much a game as a wager."

"What do you mean a wager?"

"Do you have a blindfold?"

She narrowed her eyes. "There is no way in hell I'm letting you blindfold me."

I rolled my eyes. Girls. "The blindfold is for *me*."

The rug smelled faintly of stale urine, probably from dogs. You could pick out the smell under all the years of carpet cleaner. Still, the rug was soft. I would have lain there for a while, if my reputation hadn't been on the line or if I hadn't been in agony.

"Are you hurt?" she asked.

"I don't get hurt," I said, pretty sure my ankle was broken.

"Not even after falling up a set of stairs?"

"You can't fall *up*," I said. "It's a scientific impossibility. It's the ground that's exerting its attractive force on my mass. Not the ceiling."

"Well, it really looked like you fell upward."

Rising to one knee, I felt the steps ahead of me and then slithered up the last few, reaching out in the darkness. Not being able to see was creepy, like being trapped inside a coffin, or a mine shaft, or just being blind, which wasn't exactly creepy but must be really inconvenient.

I got up, wobbling, and whipped off the stretched black sock that I'd tied over my face, blinking until I could make out the small table and laundry hamper in the upstairs hallway. "I am victorious!" I exclaimed. "I remembered enough to walk the whole house top to bottom. I told you I'd remember!"

"Well, there was that detour into the garden shed," said Gloria. "And the foot in the litter box." Then she smiled weakly. "But you did it. And I have to admit, I'm impressed, in a very weird way."

I shook my head to get rid of the dark spots lingering in my vision. We stood at the head of the stairs in front of a door with an antique crystal knob and a rusty old government sign hung on it that read BOMB SHELTER. Down the hall to the left were two other doors and another flight of stairs. "Where does that go?" I asked, pointing to the railing that curled upward into what I knew was a small third-floor space with low ceilings, because that's what it had been years ago.

"That goes to my brother's room," said Gloria, the laugh in her voice now gone. "Don't go up there," she nearly snapped.

"Okay," I said, shrugging, and then turned to the door right next to me. "Is this your room?" But she didn't need to answer, because I knew it was her bedroom. That was just how things seemed to be working out. Maybe I'd start believing in signs after all.

As we waited there, I caught a whiff of something in the hallway air, probably because I had just been blindfolded, and everyone knows that when one of your senses is dulled, the rest become heightened to superhuman levels. At least that's how it works in comics. "Do you smell smoke?" I asked.

Gloria's mouth dropped open. "You can smell that?"

"How could you not?" I said. "It's like a crematorium."

She opened the door and walked into the room, and, of course, I had no choice but to follow. Like her car, Gloria's bedroom was unexpectedly filthy, a sea of clutter with pieces of furniture occasionally rising up out of the mess like lighthouses. You could walk across the floor and never touch carpet, crossing from one end to the other on a pathway fashioned of disintegrating magazines, jewel cases, and sports bras.

Snatching a bottle of deodorizer off a tall wooden dresser by her queen-size bed, Gloria sprayed the length of her room, not even pausing to let the mist settle before squeezing another series of bursts.

"You're going to drown all the dust mites," I said.

She spun to face me, spout leveled at my face, and I flinched. "You know," she said, "I must be feeling pretty out of it, because I never let people in my bedroom, especially not strangers. Not since, like, eighth grade, when Joe Franklin was up here. And that was for a school project. And it was once."

"You're not still friends?"

"No," she said. The deodorizer nozzle dripped onto the carpet. "That was four years ago. Plus, he stole some of my mom's underwear."

I leaned against the doorjamb, hands up in innocence. "I have no interest in underwear."

"Good," she snapped.

"How well did you really know Joe Franklin, anyway?" I asked. "I mean, you and I, we've run into each other, like . . . seven times."

"*Three* times, including today," said Gloria. She tossed the spray can into one of the growing mounds of debris piling up in a corner of the room, and I half expected the junk to come alive and snatch the deodorizer out of the air midflight. Despite her orderly appearance, the girl was adorably disheveled. If you didn't look closely enough, you'd never notice that her socks didn't match or that one of the buttons on her shirt was missing, as if she'd gotten dressed in the dark. Not that she could even get to her clean clothes, since the closet door was blocked by a landfill of dirty laundry.

While most of the bedroom was a total disaster, the area around her old white wooden desk was remarkably tidy. On the surface sat a lamp, a pencil box, and a picture frame. The photo was of Gloria and a young guy, handsome, at least handsomer than me. I wondered who he was. I liked thinking that he was someone out of her past, which would explain why he was immortalized in a frame and not hanging out downstairs in her living room. Me, I was the here and now.

There was also a shabby book, a journal, the one I'd seen on her table that morning outside the coffee shop. It had flopped open, the pages overstuffed with little slips of paper, bookmarks, postcards, photos, and other scraps. I took a step closer and then began to read what was written on the page:

There is no cure
when you're not sick.

So why do I think so much,
trying to diagnose myself?
I take innocent words,
hellos, nice-to-meet-yous,
furtive glances, and untoward come-ons,
and turn them into poems—
prescriptions to cure some unknown ill.

"What's this?" I asked.

Gloria stepped up next to me and glanced around. "What?"

I read the opposite page of the journal:

From the stereo a faded love song drones.
Today I choose melancholy.
The stairs moan under each labored step.
Loads of laundry up and down,
alternating dirty and clean.
Between cycles I rearrange the bookshelves,
alphabetize the CD rack.
Time needs filling.

"Did you write these?" I asked. I couldn't imagine creating something so smart, so clear, so well thought out.

"Hey!" she snapped, and darted forward to snatch the journal off the table. I knew I'd touched a nerve, because her smooth olive cheeks turned red. "That's private."

"But it's really good," I said. "I mean *I* think so."

She looked at me. I think she was trying to figure out if I was playing a joke, if I was about to bust out laughing. "Really?" she asked. "It's just a journal. It's not important."

"If that were true, I'd be able to write something like that," I said. "And I can't. They're pretty amazing."

"Really?" she said, confused, I think. "Thanks."

I thought of how all I'd ever been capable of writing down were coordinates, the collisions of systems that most of the time made sense only to me. I was envious of how Gloria did it, how she made the feelings real. There were so few words on the paper—more would have been too many, fewer not enough. Together they perfectly communicated what she'd been thinking at the time so the reader understood even without being there. I got what she was trying to say, and as anyone who knows Charlie Wyatt can tell you, getting through to me is no easy feat.

Me, I was sort of an alien, but Gloria, she was a living, breathing human being—and an artist.

"How do you know how to do that?" I asked.

"Do what?"

"Write, like, for real, like someone would pick this book up in a store and buy it?"

"I don't know." She pressed the book to her chest like it was a treasure. "I just write what I see. You think it's good?"

I didn't think she was getting my point, that she was special. I pulled my logbook from a back pocket, its pages covered with lint, one of my hairs, and a grayish tint of dampness that smelled like sweaty jeans. I held it up so Gloria could see. "I wish I could touch people with what I do," I told her, opening the pages of my ephemerides so she could see the numerous and no doubt incomprehensible tables. "But all I know are numbers, points in the sky that are a million miles away, if not more." I sighed. "I wish I could see things like the ancients did, with imagination, with planets as gods."

I pointed down at the journal cradled in her arms, causing her to hug it tighter. "You're lucky. You make sense to people other than yourself." We faced each other across her bedroom, both of us clasping our writing to our chests. "You don't have my problem."

Her wide brown eyes clearly said "Thank you," but when she opened her mouth, she said, "I have other problems, Charlie."

We stood in the doorway, my head nearly grazing the low doorframe, and I gazed down at Gloria. She looked away, not at anything else in particular, just sort of off, away into the grungy chaos of her secret lair. I didn't know why she was so quiet. I wanted to hear what she had to say. I figured that everybody did.

"Why don't you have more friends?" I asked, setting my

logbook on the desk so I could look through some of the papers piled there. More poems. This time she didn't stop me.

She looked up at me, surprised. "What do you mean? I have friends."

"I've never seen you with anyone," I said.

"You've only seen me three times, remember?" she said. "I have friends."

I thought about this. "I hope so. You should."

Her gaze didn't waver. "Where are your friends, Charlie?"

"God knows I try," I said with a smile. That made her smile, too.

Then, sighing, she shook her head, and I don't know if it was deliberate or completely accidental, but she pushed up against me to dislodge me from her bedroom. The top of her head brushed my chin, and suddenly I was the one who felt feverish, sick in every different way at once. "Visiting hours are over," she said softly.

We spilled into the hall together, and she stepped to one side and gestured down the stairs toward the front door like a tour guide, and I knew that my time was up, just like the great Joe Franklin. Only I knew I'd be back. For one thing, I hadn't stolen any underwear, but on top of that I knew Gloria liked me, even if she hadn't figured it out yet.

MAGNET

I AWOKE WITH A START. THROWING THE SHEETS ASIDE, I LEANED far over the mattress and aimed my face down at the plastic bag. I waited. Nothing happened. That was good. My stomach felt tight, crumpled, like it had been badly packed into an overstuffed suitcase. And that was the best I'd felt all night.

Trash cans crashed to the concrete outside. I rolled over with an urge to give the garbagemen a piece of my mind. But I couldn't. Throat felt like a sandbox. Besides, I was too distracted by my mother's incessant knocking. (The rapping of knuckles does not a headache help.)

She was checking on me, again. Not surprising. I'd been damn sick.

Maggie was not pregnant. And my aches and pains hadn't been nerves. Oh no. As usual, my mother's advice had been flawed. She'd wanted me to eat, and the Chinese leftovers to boot. Well, I had. And General Tso had marched all over me. (Food poisoning: it wasn't as glamorous as the flu but thankfully shorter lived.)

Despite the sweats, the shakes, and the diarrhea—the obvious concerns—I'd been kept up all night by one single thought: Charlie Wyatt had waited outside as I'd gone to the bathroom. Me, equals mortified.

"Gloria?" said my mother softly, knocking, knocking, knocking.

"Yes?"

"You need to get up."

"Mom, I'm a chemical weapon. My body hates the world."

"That's no excuse."

"What is then?"

"You have a phone call."

"Who is it?"

"I don't recognize the name, someone Edison."

"A 'Tom,' perhaps?"

"No," she said, missing the joke, "the first name starts with a *P*."

"No idea," I said.

"Well, I'm not going to act as your answering service, so

quit lying around feeling sorry for yourself."

It was that last bit that got me out of bed. "Right, because I feel *so* sorry for myself!" I shouted, dragging my comforter up off the mattress. The sound of her departing footsteps groaned through the old house. I listened until I knew she'd gone back to her office, her fortress. Good.

But I would find no lasting peace in my bedroom. That was for sure. In fact, she'd be able to reach me anywhere in the house if she wanted to. I wrapped my puffy comforter around me like a marshmallow toga and shuffled down the steps.

Laptop and papers under my arm, I left through the side door. Then I made a beeline for the car. It took me a full ten seconds of tugging to get the whole duvet into the front seat. Getting comfortable, feet up on the dash, I unfolded my computer. Then I locked the doors. At last it was quiet again.

As my laptop booted, I stared through the windshield. Sun illuminated the dash, betraying the amount of dust that really stuck there. It was pretty disgusting. The car's interior had a faint Big Mac smell that I'd never really noticed before. On the seat between my legs was a huge splotch I'd made over Christmas vacation. I'd been trying to keep up with Maggie on the way to some state dinner. Cup balanced on the dash, I'd taken a corner fast. Down came the latte, syrup and all. I hadn't even bothered to clean it up afterward.

For some strange reason, I felt like trying now. Better late than never, I guess.

Leaning over, I felt around under my seat. My fingers found the small plastic container of wipes almost instantly. It sat where it always did, wedged up against the tiny travel trash can. Not that I'd ever used either. It was Faris who had stashed the supplies there. I'm convinced he put them in on the very day he bought the car. He was anal that way, meaning he cared for things.

I pulled out the container and the can. Then I popped the lid off the special auto-care wipes. The smell was strong, clean. It cut the sour stench like a shaft of light in a dark room. Not once in the last year had I taken out a wipe. Not once had I cleaned my brother's car.

I hated clean. It was too much work. I'd never forget how Faris spent a few minutes every morning before school hunched over the driver's side, door open, gunning the minivac. He loved that car. Me, I treated it like a bottomless pit.

A sharp stab of sadness paralyzed me in my seat. I couldn't bear to be in my own body, to be me. I thought I missed my brother so much, and here I couldn't fork over fifteen dollars on a car wash for his prized possession. I was such a huge bitch.

Faris bought the Toyota with his own money. (He could have just waited until Mom got around to buying him one. That's what I'd been planning to do. Not my brother.) He delivered papers. He mowed lawns. He walked dogs. He worked at the local pharmacy (à la Charlie Wyatt) back when the place was called Hoffman's. Not once did he ask for help.

I checked myself. Why had I just thought about Charlie Wyatt?

It didn't matter. Reaching across the dash, I very slowly wiped a path through the dust. The cloth left a dazzling gray trail behind it, like new.

On my third pass I caught a look at myself in the rearview mirror. My black hair hung wavy in front of my face. It always did that in the heat and after days without washing. I couldn't help but recall when my hair had been strawberry blond and I refused to wear black because it was "depressing." Now the only light was at my roots.

So much had changed.

I started to cough uncontrollably and had to put down the wipe to cover my face. My body apparently felt the need to make more pollutants for the already contaminated car. When the hacking stopped, I took a deep breath. Breathe, I told myself. Breathe.

I flopped back in my seat and stared outside. That tiny

patch of car interior I'd cleaned caught the sunlight—flashed. It was so small, downright pitiful.

There was no way in hell I'd be able to get rid of all the crap, start over. The car was a lost cause. It was caked in a year's worth of filth, and then some. No matter how much I scrubbed or how many expensive wipes I used, it would stay a mess. Period.

As I lay there, bloblike, my phone rang from where it lay on my laptop. It vibrated. I turned to watch it dance but didn't answer. The caller ID flashed: EDISON, PAUL again and again. There was no denying it. I was curious.

After four rings, the phone rattled itself right off the computer to the floor of the car, where it turned in a circle between two empty Sprite cans.

That was it. I picked up.

I pressed the button. "Hello."

"Yeah, hi," said the distant, pinched voice on the other end. I couldn't hear him well. There were people arguing in the background, boys. "Is this Gloria?"

"Yes," I said in a slightly bitchy voice. "Is this Paul Edison?"

"Actually, no," said the guy. "Wait . . . how do you know this is Edison's phone?"

"Ever hear of caller ID?" I said. "You're not much of a genius, Edison," I went on. "Listen, you've been trying me all morning, and I'm pretty sure you have the wrong number. Check your information. Bye-bye."

I waited for the hang-up, but it didn't come. Instead, the boy moved someplace quieter, where his voice could finally be heard. Then he spoke directly into the receiver for the first time. "Gloria, it's me."

I nearly dropped the phone.

"Hello?" he said. And I heard that familiar intensity. That Charlie sound. "Gloria, is that you?" The voice jumped from the holes in the plastic. It hung in the air like a spirit at a séance.

"Charlie?" I said hesitantly.

"Gloria?" Oh yeah, it was him, all right.

"What the hell, Charlie?" I said, both annoyed and glad to hear his voice. "I didn't answer. Can't you take a hint? I'm busy, and I don't feel like talking."

"Why? Are you writing?"

I sighed. "No, I'm not writing. I might if I ever get off the phone. How did you get this number, anyway?"

"I took it off your phone when you went to the bathroom. Remember, at the store, you asked me to hold your shit. That's how you put it."

"Right," I said, mentally kicking myself. "Charlie, why does your phone come up as Paul Edison's?"

"Edison's my friend," he said. "He's got a bunch of phones

and a couple numbers. So he gave me one. Of course, I never figured out how to switch all the info stuff to my name."

"So you walk around pretending to be Paul Edison."

"Well, he can't walk because he's in a wheelchair, but I see what you meant."

I sighed. "Listen, Charlie, I've gotta go."

"Oh. Okay."

"Maybe I'll see you later though."

I realized my mistake a second too late. "You'll see me later?" he asked, voice full of excitement.

"I said 'maybe.'"

I could hear his smile through the phone. "Maybe?" he said. "That could mean yes." And then, just as startlingly as he'd called, he was gone.

He was too bizarre. It required noting.

After everything—talking to Mom, memories of Faris, and the call from Charlie—I needed to get some writing done. It was time to clear my mind. (No more distractions.) Rooting through my stack of crumpled papers and laptop wires, I found my Freak Folio and picked it up. I removed the pink rubber band. (Distractions, be gone!) As I cracked the binding and smelled the familiar smell of the paper (coffee and hand lotion), a small black something slid out of the pages. It landed on the seat cushion with a thump.

Distractions!

It was a small black logbook about the size of a TV remote. The cover was bent and doodled on and looked to have been chewed off in a corner.

Opening a stranger's journal is like steaming someone's mail, and I felt a tingle of excitement and fear as I thumbed the first few pages. Once upon a time they'd been white. Now they were a sweaty yellow. The empty space was filled with scrawls of handwriting I didn't recognize and mathematical tables:

Name	Right Ascension	Declination	Altitude	Start Time
Dorothy	00:12:25	+30:04:00	-09:00	A.D. 2009-Jun-21
				00:00:00.0000 UT

It was a language I did not speak, utterly alien.

One name—and one name only—came to mind.

Twenty minutes later, I sat in a parking space staring at a store window. Someone had spray painted the words "Come, See Our Silly Summer Savings!" on the glass. Rain fell lightly through the sunlight.

I didn't want to talk to Charlie. Not really. I mean, I didn't have anything particular to say to him. Every once in a while I just felt lonely. (People don't need to speak to be together, right?)

What I liked about Charlie was that he didn't know me at all. Not like other people did. He wasn't always asking me if I was okay, if I was feeling better. He had a whole other point of view and took me for who I was in the moment. Sure, I didn't quite understand why things worked this way, but that was okay. I think he sought me out for the very same reason. Neither of us knew why we got along. We just seemed to.

With a loud groan as a warning, the passenger side door swung open. (Sometimes it seemed like people tracked me down faster in the car. That was a problem because the whole reason I'd started hanging out there was to escape.) I smelled the scent of my sister's overpowering perfume. Then I heard the shrill sound of her Nintendo powering down. Stealthy, Maggie was not. A girl who wears tube tops and a fedora when she's getting her morning coffee is not one for sneak attacks.

Her head appeared sideways in the open door. She popped her gum twice. "You know we're both health hazards, right?" she said. "Or did you miss the news flash? Oh, and you might want to avoid Kowloon Kingdom for a while." She thought of something and smiled. "Maybe we should see if Mom wants to hire them to cater her big dinner. Award for the fastest dash to the can goes to . . . the United Arab Emirates."

"You're gross," I said. "Go away. I'm running errands."

"You must be making great time with the emergency brake

on." She looked up at Family Friends pharmacy and then back at me. "Running low on SSRIs?"

"Yup," I said, lying. "Here I am, out of meds again."

She slid in next to me in the car. "You could have just called. I was fetching caffeine. Probably not good for the stomach, but oh well. Want me to get them?"

"No."

If she ever found out that I was stalking Charlie, I'd never hear the end of it.

I needed to put an end to the conversation. Opening the door, I stepped out into the hot day. My puffy comforter trailed behind me. I wasn't going anywhere without my security blanket. Not with the chills I was still having.

I turned back for one last witty comment, but Maggie had already popped her buds back into her ears. As she did, she said, "Good thing you got the blanket. I can see your panty line. That means so can everyone else." Sighing, I left my sister—and my dignity—and headed inside, Charlie's tattered logbook under one arm.

The sliding doors dinged when I entered. A couple of young guys in red vests stood behind the counter. They whacked each other with rolled-up copies of *People*. For a second I wondered if all of Family Friends' employees were as strange as Charlie Wyatt. But I knew better than that.

I walked up to the taller of the guys. He appeared the more

serious of the two. He had bug eyes and spindly fingers. Like some kind of half man, half lemur.

"Is Charlie here?" I asked him. His name tag said ARNOLD.

"No," said Arnold. "Charlie's not working today."

"Well, do you know where he is?"

"Probably at his house," said the other guy. This kid was ridiculously tiny. He had a puffy hairdo that looked like it had risen in an oven.

"I have to give him something. Where's he live?"

"I don't think I should give out that information," said Arnold, the lemur man.

"Come on," I said. "I'm not the gestapo. Look at me. I'm wearing a duvet."

"You can leave a note," said Arnold. "I'll make sure he gets it."

"I'm not leaving a note," I said, growing irritable. I pointed down at the little guy, whose name tag said TOMMY. "What about him, does he know?"

"That's Little Tommy," said Arnold the lemur. "He's busy."

"Busy what, breathing?"

"Charlie lives over in the Soleil Day Apartments, off Lee Highway. Down by the sixty-six overpass." Little Tommy had spoken. He stared at us, eyelids so droopy he could have been asleep.

I grinned victoriously at Arnold. He just shook his head.

"Thanks," I said to Little Tommy. But he'd already gone back to shooting items with a price gun: $325.00 for a box of Kleenex; $999.99 for a tube of toothpaste.

When I squeezed back into the car, comforter and all, Maggie was waiting. She watched my every move, an arm curled around a headrest. Her suspicious gaze reminded me of our mother's— speaking volumes without a word. (Maggie would have lost it if she'd known how much she resembled Mom. The two shared the same stare but didn't see eye to eye on anything.)

I sat. She stared. I put the keys in the ignition. She stared.

"Just say it!" I shouted, throwing my hands in the air.

Laughing triumphantly, she flicked one of my ears. "What are you doing?"

"What do you mean?"

"Exactly what it sounds like," she said. "Why are you driving around with day-old makeup on, interrogating guys at the pharmacy?"

When I didn't respond, she ran her fingers through my greasy, sick person's hair. "I don't like to act big sisterly very often, because, honestly, I don't know any more than you do about anything. In fact, I probably know less than you do about everything." She smiled. I loved Maggie. We were so different; but not.

"I'm hardly smarter than you," I said.

"You know you are and that's okay," she said, winking.

"That's not important. What *is* important is that because you're special, I want to take care of you. That's what big sisters do, okay?"

"Okay?" I wasn't sure where she was going with this.

Then she grew serious, a Maggie rarity. "I'm sorry about yesterday," she said. "I lost my shit, and I don't like to lose my shit, Glory. Sometimes I screw up big. I know that everybody thinks that's my thing—to screw up—but the whole pregnancy-scare thing, well, that was primo. I guess even a little girl like me needs a reality check every once in a while."

"You're not a screwup," I said, touching her arm. "You're a dollface."

She shrugged. "Well, Pill is history."

"I've heard that before," I murmured.

"Shut up," she said. "Besides, I could care less about that. What bothered me most was how you had to watch out for me, and that's not the arrangement."

"It's not, huh?"

"No," she said. "And because it's my job to guide you, I'm tagging along on whatever adventure you've cooked up for the day."

I arched an eyebrow. "Aren't you supposed to dissuade me from acting crazy?"

"Well, normally I would," she said. "I'd watch amusedly as whatever you're doing spins out of control and blows up in your face. Not today, though."

"Why not today?" I asked.

"Because," she said as I started the engine, "you're acting crazy." That wink again. "And nobody needs crazy more than you do."

I leaned over and kissed my sister on the cheek. "Love you," I said.

"I love you, too," she told me. "Now who are we pestering next?"

We almost missed the sign for the Soleil Day Apartments. I swerved left into its potholed driveway in the nick of time. It was a series of bland complexes hugging the Virginia side of the Potomac River. Saturday traffic was backed up on the bridge leading into Georgetown. A coming thunderstorm hadn't yet broken over the blue.

"So what's the plan?" asked Maggie.

"Beats me," I said.

Maggie raised a finger. "Is that your guy?" She nodded forward through the windshield. I looked where she was pointing. (I'd explained to her about Charlie, just enough so she'd stay with me as backup, but not enough for any real, meaty gossip. She knew exactly who he was, as she'd been to the pharmacy before and had noticed him. She had deemed him surprisingly foxy for someone so awkward and

even had a nickname for him: "my Family Friend fantasy."
As usual, my sister was a disgusting lecher.)

Outside the apartment entrance and past the outdoor ash-
trays was a small courtyard. Ragged topiaries lined the path. A
sundial rusted in a pit of bone-white gravel. There beside one
of the benches sat a woman in a wheelchair. She sat slumped,
head drooped forward, arms on the cushioned rests. On her
face was the biggest smile I'd ever seen—a lazy half-moon of
teeth in the afternoon sun.

Charlie sat next to the woman in a rainbow lawn chair
with a very saggy seat. He pointed at the sky and talked inces-
santly. She responded but only after long stretches of silence.
Her answers were never more than a word or two.

Maggie glanced at me. "I've bought stuff from him before.
He kept recommending things I hadn't asked about. He
cracked me up. Hot and weird, that's just my type."

"Yeah," I murmured. "Keep your slutty hands off."

She made a feral cat sound. Ha. Ha.

"Is that his mom?"

"I don't know."

"They look pretty happy."

"Yeah."

"Something just occurred to me."

"What?"

She raised an eyebrow. "This is your first stalking, isn't it?"

I made a face. She made a cat sound again. It wasn't funny the first time.

We watched them for what felt like a long time. Then the storm broke, and the sky filled with shadow. As I started the car, I watched Charlie fold up the lawn chair. He held it over the lady's head to keep her safe from the rain. Its seat sagged so badly, I'm surprised his butt hadn't grazed the ground. Knowing Charlie—which I think I was starting to—I guessed he'd spent the morning jumping on it.

"Pull me up to the entrance," I said.

"Are you going in?" she asked, amazed.

"Maybe," I said.

Reaching into my pocket, I took out Charlie's small black logbook. It's funny. I didn't want to let go of it. I liked how I had something that belonged to him.

I plucked a red pen from the car ashtray, removed the cap. My hand shook. With jerky movements, I flipped open the logbook's front cover and wrote. Then it was done.

"Don't you dare go anywhere," I said to Maggie as I cracked the door.

"You kidding?" she said. "I wouldn't miss this for the world."

FREAK

"IS EVERYTHING ALL RIGHT?"

It took me several seconds to focus and then shift to Dad, who smeared apple butter on one of his English muffins before folding the crispy circle in half and biting into it like a sandwich. "You seem a little sleepy," he said. "Spent too long at the telescope last night?" It was Saturday, and the sky rumbled with a thunderstorm. NPR murmured from the radio under the kitchen cabinets, and the guy who lived upstairs clonked around in what sounded like army boots. I think he was a cage fighter, or at least that's what the doorman told me that time he showed up high to work the front desk.

"No, not sleepy," I said, wiping my mouth on the sleeve of

my flannel pajamas. "I'm just thinking." I didn't want to tell him that I hadn't tracked my comet the night before because of a lost logbook that was likely on some girl's bedroom floor mixed in with her bras. That was just too scandalous to get into over waffles.

"Thinking, huh?" he said, laughing, and he bit into his muffin again—*chomp!* "I don't want to know."

Across the table, Mom's droopy eyes rested on my face, like they had all through the meal. Her hair looked really nice. She and I had washed it that morning, spending the extra half hour to blow it dry. After we'd finished, she'd managed "thank you" when I wasn't expecting it, as she was peeing on the toilet and I was sitting outside the cracked door waiting to help her back to her feet again.

Sometimes I wish she said more. I'd told her all about my trip to Gloria's house and how we'd connected; and while I was grateful that she couldn't lecture me on the rudeness of not leaving a young girl's house when she first asked me to—which she certainly would have, had she possessed the energy—I still yearned for more of a reaction, for guidance on how to deal with teenage girls, considering she'd been one once and might have some insight into the subject.

To me, girls were like newly discovered planets. You could determine only so much about them with the available information. Was the atmosphere around them breathable? I have no idea! Was the surface hospitable to new life? Who knows? Would getting too close to them kill you? Probably! There were just too many questions.

I stared at my mom and then back at Dad, who was having a jolly time ingesting.

"How did you meet each other?" I asked.

Dad found the *Washington Post* crossword puzzle and was soon lost in the grid. "How did who meet each other?"

"You and Mom," I said.

"We had a mutual friend," he said. He still wasn't paying much attention to the conversation, raising his coffee cup to his lips.

"No," I said. "How did you, like, *meet*? When did you know she was special?"

The newspaper dropped a few inches, enough so that I could see the spark in his blue eyes. "I've never told you?" he asked with a smile.

"Like I would forget," I said.

"True," he said, and dropped the newspaper to the table. "You're not exactly the forgetting type." He slid his baseball cap back and forth on his balding head, the telltale sign of his excitement. As he did, our upstairs neighbor stomped on our heads, lunging, perhaps, or maybe practicing his grapples.

Dad sat thinking, gaze on the bull's-eye logo of his coffee mug—a vinyl-siding company with the motto: "We've got you covered." It gave him a fixed point to stare at, a target other than me. I rarely saw my father so dreamy, and it reminded me of the time I saw him get drunk one New Year's day when some of his old buddies dropped by to give him their leftover liquor. That January 1 he'd drunk alone, for hours, listening to CDs, slowly drifting off into some negative zone where everything was as it'd been in 1978, and he was a football star with all his hair and had a girlfriend who didn't need an adult diaper.

"Earth to Wyatt," I said.

"Sorry," he said, that spark still in his eyes. "That was a good year." He cast a glance at my mother as he got up from his chair to refresh his coffee. "We met after a football game," he continued. "Your mother was a sophomore and I was a senior. She came to most of the games, and then one night some of the cheerleaders invited her to go out with us afterward. The rest of the guys went out for beers, but your mom and me, we said no. We went and got ice cream."

"You got ice cream?" I said skeptically.

"Yeah," he said.

"Was it the big homecoming game?" I asked.

"No. I think we played Fairfax—and lost."

"You *lost*? Was she new in town? Was she like a transfer student or something?"

"No. Actually, I had a class with her brother, just didn't know it."

"Had you guys known each other as kids?"

"I don't think so. No one ever said we did, so it never crossed my mind."

I sat quietly, considering the factors involved. From what I could figure, passion blossomed from incredible coincidence that most often was mistaken for fate; this made sense to me. Probability dictated that certain human variables, when combined, would result in feelings of attraction between pairs of people, of a euphoric feeling of connectedness otherwise known as "destiny." But this usually wore off, as that spark faded, only to be replaced by a similar chemistry with a new individual.

However, the inconsistency, the true variable, was in the exceptions to the rule: when couples stayed together and the light burned brightly for a lifetime without diminishing. How were those cases different? Was there something bigger at work? Was I going crazy?

"It's not too exciting a story," said Dad, watching me. "Not like the movies."

"But it is," I said, tapping my chin. "What were the odds that Superman would get a job at the same newspaper where Lois Lane worked? You see my point?"

At that, Dad sort of laughed. "I'm hardly Superman." He spooned sugar into his mug and then stirred. "And your mom's a lot prettier than Lois Lane." He gave her a wink.

Leaning back in my chair, I began to crack my knuckles

very slowly, one after another. "I wonder if there's more to love than I expected, if, like, it's not governed by the same rules. When I meet a girl and it's special, will I know it?"

Seconds ago, Dad had been lost in nostalgia, but now he was sort of grinning again. "I guess that's something to think about," he said. Then suddenly he seemed to realize where all this was coming from and cocked an eyebrow mischievously. "Why? *Is* there a girl?"

"No," I said, lying.

"You're lying," he said, calling my bluff.

Then, as if on cue, Mom leaned forward in her wheelchair and opened her mouth to speak, her beautiful hair sliding down the length of her pale neck. Her teeth had become crooked in the last few years, and her lips were almost always dried like crepe paper. Dad and I leaned in, listening. There was no noise at first. Then . . .

"Let the boy have his secrets," she said at last.

Dad grumbled. I grinned.

What can I say? I'm a mama's boy.

I shut my bedroom door behind me and flopped face-first onto my bedspread in my pajamas, holding out my arms like wings, as if I could bounce right back up and take flight, like one of those acrobats in that fancy French circus with the black lights and techno music, only not as high, since I was afraid of heights, and not just the big ones but all of them.

Getting up, I sat on the edge of the mattress and peered through the eyepiece of my Maksutov, the telescope I'd bought several years ago with my own money—and lots of it. But I wasn't really interested in gazing that evening, which was rare.

After a few minutes at the Maksutov, I got down on my hands and knees on the floor and peered into the darkness beneath my bed, feeling around under the bed frame until I found the brown shipping box where I first stashed it nearly eight months ago. I pulled it out, opened it, and dug through the remaining puffy packing peanuts. In the middle of the flat cardboard sat my superpower, now crumpled and in need of a washing, nothing like when I received it in the mail from someone calling himself gohero991@hothollywood.com. When I unfolded the tights, they released a much riper smell than cologne. They had the scent of invulnerability. That or butt sweat.

In my hands I held my suit: an exact replica of the Superman costume used in the classic Richard Donner movies, at least those that were considered classics, as in *Superman* and *Superman II*. I'd gotten the outfit from a movie prop ware-house on the internet, and ended up spending four hundred and fifty dollars of my grandfather's inheritance to win the auction.

Every year Edison and I attend the Baltimore Comic-Con,

a big brouhaha up in Charm City to the north. Last year, he'd suggested we dress up, something we'd managed to avoid doing for a long time, as it would officially mark us as genre fanboys, a particular race of people I did not associate with in the least. He wanted to distract me, to break me out of the funk I'd been drowning in. I understood his concern. I was in a bad way.

After years of caring for a parent, you start to forget the years when they cared for you. It's not an easy transition to make. You realize that while the past may live on in memory, memories most certainly fade, as is their nature.

So Edison and I showed up at the convention in the guise of our favorite characters. He wore a bald cap and went as Professor X from *X-Men*, which was a no-brainer since renting a wheelchair can be pricey and, while Edison's chair didn't hover like the professor's fictional version, it was pretty darn swanky. My choice of character was also a given. I didn't care for any other comic books but the various Superman titles, so I searched the internet for outfits and found myself becoming oddly consumed with the task, never committing until I found a suit that was as authentic as possible—thus the four hundred and fifty dollars, plus shipping and handling.

That day in Baltimore with Edison, the sky was clear, the sun was high and hot and a pure bold yellow, as if we really had strolled off the dingy streets of life into the rainbow panels of a comic book. I met Klingons and a group of girls dressed as Japanese cartoon vampires, and we had our picture taken dueling with light sabers, and I laughed—I laughed more than I had in weeks. Most of all, I remembered: There was life away from my telescope, and outside my bedroom door, and beyond the 1970s concrete styling of our rundown apartment building that my dad spent his days trying to repair. There was more.

And so I kept wearing it.

Every single day I cloaked myself in that clingy layer like it was a bulletproof vest. I'd worn it under my regular clothes whenever I left the house—at school, during work, out with Edison—for 236 days straight. Since that time, no additional tragedy had struck, and I felt better, positive. Maybe I was crazy. But is it crazy to keep doing the one thing that has ever worked?

Hurrying, in case my dad knocked—or worse, just came in—I slipped into the costume, which was like a hug, one that never ended. It made me look big, sturdy, and I felt bigger and sturdier wearing it.

Behind me, the bedroom door creaked open. I pulled on my gray long-sleeved T-shirt just in time; Dad wandered in a moment later, as he often did, without any form of warning. He didn't look at me. His face was turned down toward a stack of mail that he flipped through with a beefy index finger.

"Check this out," he said, and snatched something from the pile.

In his hands he held my small black logbook, the one that I'd thought was lost. Crossing the room, I took it from him and hurriedly flipped through the pages, wanting to make sure everything was right where it should be. Everything was. I breathed a deep sigh of relief . . . until a flash of red caught my eye. I turned to the front cover, which was nearly coming off in a mess of cracked and brittle cardboard.

Written on the back were the words: *"I like how you see the world. Gloria. P.S. Get a new notebook."*

It was a sign.

MAGNET

NO. THERE IS NOTHING AT ALL NATURAL ABOUT THE HIGH HEEL. It's been proven. It's anthropological. The high heel is simply a tool intended to elevate the female form in a certain way so as to make it more attractive to males. (Not that they need any help in that department, the perverts.) Posture on the heel positions the frame in such a way that a woman's breasts and backside become more pronounced. It's like going the extra mile to stuff a turkey when you know that people are going to eat it anyway.

More importantly, heels hurt like hell, and I can't walk in them to save my life.

Nevertheless, I wore them. You couldn't try on a dress

without making sure the shoes matched. That would be like driving a car without making sure it had tires first. I posed, modeling the dress . . . and hating it. Cher blasted from the speakers overhead. It was a song from her "terrible" phase—meaning all of them. I turned on the heels, all the while dreaming of flip-flops.

We were at Macy's, and I was hiding from my mother. She was off in another part of the store. It had become her quest to find me something to wear to her foundation's awards dinner in a few weeks. I hadn't even agreed to go yet and was only just barely feeling human again. That's how hopeful she was. Of course, I had to agree to an outfit first. That was the arrangement. And I didn't do formal.

"Are you listening to me?" Maggie asked. She grabbed the dressing room door and hoisted her body up. Then she gazed down at me, her hair in pigtails.

"So, Pill wants to be exclusive?" I asked, interested but busy.

"Long-distance, to be precise," she said.

"When you go back to school?"

"Right-o."

"But you don't do long-distance."

"A fact he knows all too well."

"Sounds like he wants to get serious," I said.

She scratched at the door and whispered, "Spooky, no?"

"Horrifying," I said, but then shrugged. "Perhaps it's time for Kiki Dash to retire her vinyl hot pants and settle down."

The door opened. Maggie stuck one arm into the crack. "You're a hoot," she said, rattling a hanger. The crème-colored gown swayed. "And about this little number, we feel . . . ?"

"Yuck," I said.

She switched hangers. The next dress dangled with black beads and spangles. It would have looked at home on a 1920s cocktail waitress. "Or . . . ?"

"Or puke," I said.

"Yuck and puke," said Maggie. "Must be the food poisoning talking." She shuffled off to comb the racks for more options.

"I'M MUCH BETTER NOW!" I called, probably too loudly.

It was a very Charlie Wyatt thing to do.

It could have been a great weekend. Maggie and I had planned to spend the day shopping in Georgetown—just the two of us. But Mom had switched her plans and inserted herself into our afternoon. It was like we were a ship and she was a pirate. She swung right over our bow, a sword between her teeth. "I don't want to be a nuisance," she said. All the while directing us to stores she wanted and ignoring our suggestions.

I listened to Maggie leave, knowing she wasn't going to

find anything I liked. (After all, she was a twenty-year-old woman wearing a Catholic schoolgirl's uniform and a plastic pink backpack.) When it came to fashion, Maggie didn't fit the requirements of Macy's ladies' department. Like everything else, she had a category all her own.

Gazing down at the gold heel, I remembered when I used to get off on clothes. That was little more than a year ago. My world had been the four square feet behind the door of a dressing room. Life was all about showing the world a glossy package. Like Mom always did. Everything was orderly. Everything was perfect. Or so it seemed. Something always happens to remind you of how little control we really have. Sometimes that something is your brother's death.

Before it happened, my hair was lighter, styled. I wore only enough makeup to bring out my eyes. I was a clotheshorse. I was a princess. I was weak. After it happened, I wore my hair black, because it went with everything. I liked it best when the mascara was so dark it looked like I didn't have eyes. There are just two holes where my eyes used to be.

Still, I had to admit that the gold heels were pretty. A year ago I would have loved them. Now they just hurt. I tossed them onto the floor.

"How's it going out there?" I asked through the door.

No response.

"Maggie?"

"Right here."

"Anything?"

"I'm coming up with nothing," she said, followed by a pause.

I threw open the door and stuck out my head. Maggie sat on a sofa reading an issue of *Ghost Rider*. She hadn't even ventured as far as the sash and scarf rack. The groan of the door hinges tipped her off. She spun around, a sheepish "hand-in-the-cookie-jar" grin on her face.

"Thanks for the help," I said sarcastically.

"Hey, you have your little book of secrets, and I have this stuff," she said. "Give me a break. It's my kryptonite."

When she said that, something occurred to me. It showed plainly on my face.

"What?" Maggie asked, worried.

"My journal," I said. "I left it at home."

"So?" she said.

"So I don't like to go places without it."

She shook her head and went back to *Ghost Rider*. "If you feel that naked, there's a dressing room right behind you." Then she made a *tsk-tsk* sound. "Artists."

Fifteen minutes later, my sister and I loitered in cosmetics. The exotic smell of mixing perfumes hung over our heads. We had to talk a little louder than usual to be heard over the squeaking of hangers and the pop music. We circled the main counter, arms linked. Mom was nowhere to be seen.

I looked down at our two wrists. It was impossible not to notice how Maggie had already turned a deep cinnamon from the summer sun. You'd think she'd just returned from spring break. Her wide brown eyes sparkled. As always, a slight powdering of glitter stuck to her cheeks. She was a knockout, even having gone three days without bathing.

All my life I had been jealous of Maggie's beauty. How had she ended up with more of our mother's looks than I had? We both got along with her in equally dysfunctional ways. It wasn't fair.

"Stop looking at me like that," she said suddenly.

"Like what?"

"Like you're about to cry," she said. "I know what you're thinking, because you've thought it since we were kids, and it's not true. I'm not the one romancing the red-vested stud in Aisle Whatever."

"You'd better shut up right now," I said. "I'm not interested in Charlie."

"Ha," she said, laughing. "You're celibate now, but last year was a different story. You would have gotten kicked out of a brothel, sister."

The problem with siblings is that you can have the same argument with them for ten years and still not make any progress on it. In my eyes, all the kids in our family had roles to play. Maggie had always been the beautiful one. Me, I was the sensitive one. Faris, he'd been the responsible one. No doubt the two of them had seen things differently. The point was that I wasn't the beautiful one.

Maggie constantly tried to convince me that I wasn't unattractive; but walking around next to her made me ugly—or *uglier*. At least that's how it felt.

She looked away. "I think a boyfriend would do you some good."

"Yeah, well, I don't know what to think," I said.

"You think too much," said Maggie. "That's your problem. Always has been."

Her grip on my arm tightened as she pulled me off the path. She stopped at a pair of tables alongside the escalators that led upstairs. It was a collection of discount merchandise. On a lonely metal rack hung a few spring outfits that were already out of style for the coming fall. A metal sign in the center of the table declared: "Seasonal Slashes: Everything 50% Off List Price." Maggie began shuffling through the hangers on the nearly bare rack. There were sundresses, cute, with light colors. A few of them sprouted head to toe with flowers.

"I don't think too much," I said. "Sometimes it's just better than feeling everything. Thinking about things makes them less painful, distant or something."

"I understand," she said, examining the clothes.

Maggie tugged a dress free from the tangle. It was simple, white with yellow embroidered petals circling the hem. It was cheerful. (I didn't hate it. That was a start.)

"That's why you keep that journal," she said. "Because it helps you process everything, instead of carrying it around."

"You think?" I asked.

Maggie slipped the straps off the hanger. She draped the dress over my chest and took a second look. Like she was the mom and I was the kid. The hem hung down to just a few inches below the knee. "Sure," she added, still talking as she went about playing dress-up. "You write down how you feel. It gives you space, helps you to separate." She paused. "You keep people at a distance. But sometimes you push them away, like you're angry at anyone who tries to be happy."

"That's not true," I protested, maybe too much.

Still holding up the dress, she spun a small rack of earrings on the nearby table. The collection of cheap jewelry tinkled as it turned. "It's okay. I know you don't hate *me*," she said. "That would be unheard of. But some days you push me away, too. Not all days, just the bad ones."

Gasping, she stopped the whirling plastic rack. A pair of small amber pendants glittered. Maggie plucked them from their slots and held them to my ears. "Beautiful," she said, pursing her lips cutely.

It was all she managed, classic Maggie—everything was breathtaking, amazing, or incredible. It was a lot to live up to.

"Whatever," I said.

"No, really," she continued. "You look like a model."

"Don't mess with me," I said, almost snapping.

Why all the drama? Couldn't I just be not-ugly?

"There, that's it," she said, a wan smile appearing. "That's the Gloria I'm not so fond of."

"What does that mean?" I stepped back, grabbing the dress away.

"Always on the defensive," she said. "Fight or flight. In your case, they're kind of the same, first the fight, and then the flight, and usually to the car." She took back the dress and smoothed it out again. "Babe, anyone who tries to get too close gets bitten."

I knew she was right. I couldn't deal. Not with intimacy. Acting that way was cold. And it wasn't me. At least not how I saw myself, or wanted to. But I couldn't seem to change it.

"Maggie, am I that way with everyone?"

"Not everyone." Her cheerful expression became gravely serious. The effect was incredible. When someone who is always smiling doesn't, you realize how unrecognizable they are without that one defining feature. "Mostly just Mom," she said.

I didn't know what to say.

Maggie removed the whole outfit and folded it up for purchase. "Glory, if I didn't know better, I'd think you hated her guts," she said. Then she walked to the register.

Alone by the escalators, I should have pondered my mother, or Faris. Or even Maggie and how I despised her dark curls, curves, and legs. But I didn't. I thought about Charlie Wyatt.

I thought about that day he chewed me out at the Grind House. He'd said something similar: that I didn't give people a chance. Maybe he was right. Maybe they all were. You can't push people away forever. Eventually you'll run out of people to shove.

Clearance items lay around me on the dark wooden display. There were golf balls and an assortment of shiny wallets. A battery-operated shoe buffer sat in a mashed cardboard box. Piles of faded handkerchiefs leaned unwanted against the wall. Everything was marked with the yellow tag of the near worthless. Only one item stood out from the rest.

It was a small journal. It was nice, leather. It might even have wound up on the table by accident.

I thought about Charlie and the scribbled writings he kept in that ratty logbook of his. The pages were falling out. The cover was practically nonexistent. If anyone could use a new place to keep his thoughts, it was him. I'd told him as much in my note.

"Did you find something?" asked a hopeful voice.

I looked up into my mother's deep blue mascara. Like a pool you'd be afraid to enter without a life preserver.

FREAK

GRASPING THE TOP OF THE LADDER, I HANDED THE CUSTOMER THE box of laxatives.

Below me, she appeared small, frail, like I could have crushed her with the heel of my shoe, and the more I thought about it, the more I wondered if she appeared *too* small. This possibility unsettled me, and as soon as I had surrendered the laxative, I second-guessed myself and wished I hadn't.

"You don't have an eating disorder, do you?"

"Excuse me?" she said. I tried to determine if she was "thin" or "skinny," and if she was "skinny" was she "*too* skinny"? I guessed she was a nurse, because she wore a shirt that had no collars and no buttons, and had a pattern consisting of little cartoon honeybees. No one but a nurse would ever wear something like that out of the house.

"Well," I said, "as you probably know, being a part of the medical profession, a lot of women use laxatives to control their consumption. That way, you can keep eating and still get rid of food quickly. If that's what you're planning to do, I'd like you to give back the box, because I don't want to be responsible for that sort of thing."

"Go to hell," said the woman.

I nodded, cursing my stupidity. "Okay then. Thanks for coming to Family Friends." Once again, I'd gone about ten steps too far in trying to relate. Clearly I wasn't going to be up for a promotion anytime soon.

Sighing, I arranged a few boxes of those headache medicine sticks that you roll across your forehead like lip balm. From my perch on the ladder atop Aisle Three, I watched the nurse stand at the cash register and talk with Mr. Pastore. She looked angry, and he looked pale and sweaty, which was actually pretty normal. If the guy hadn't looked pasty and about to faint, I'd have started to worry.

As soon as the woman had left the store—without purchasing anything, I might add—Mr. Pastore walked toward me, his shirttails hanging out of the back of his waistband. His tie hung crooked, like the hand of a watch at four o'clock. He stopped at the foot of my ladder, looking up at me. Like the woman, he was a tiny speck. "What did we talk about, Charlie?" he said. "Customer service, that's how we stay in business."

"She looked shady," I said, trying to cover my ass. "I think she may have been a shoplifter."

A small smile appeared on his face. "She's my neighbor, Charlie. I explained to her that you were practicing to be a stand-up comic. Needless to say, she didn't find you very funny."

"She's not the only one," I said. "That's strike three for the day, sir."

He gestured toward the rear of the store. "Are you sure you don't want to work in back, take inventory? You wouldn't have to worry about all the face time."

"I don't like it back there," I said. "No windows. Can't see . . ." And I pointed up at the ceiling.

He nodded knowingly. "Would you do me a favor, Charlie?"

"Depends on the favor," I said.

That made him smile. "I need someone to cover the night shift tonight, the seven to ten, and none of the other guys want to do it."

"Isn't Lawrence coming in?" I asked.

"I have no idea," said Mr. Pastore. "I haven't heard from Lawrence in a week."

"That's *so* Lawrence," I said, shaking my head. My

rotund fellow Customer Service Associate was known for his lengthy absences—and his love of sniffing glue with his punk rock girlfriend, Janice.

"You've only been here for an hour," said Mr. Pastore. "Leave now, spend the day outside, and then come back in the evening. I'll pay you for the full shift."

I scratched my chin. It was quite the proposition. "You're on," I said.

"You're a lifesaver, Charlie," he said with a sigh. Then he looked at me funny, as if for the first time. "Are you feeling okay? You look a little tired. Even more than usual, I mean. Up all night thinking about the big trip?"

"Always," I said. But I wasn't.

I'd been thinking about Gloria.

She hadn't gotten back in touch with me. I'd called her on Edison's phone a week ago, we'd talked for maybe thirty seconds before she had to hang up, and when she had, I'd gotten the clear impression that we'd finish the conversation later. That had never happened. I didn't like radio silence. Nothing makes a person feel more alone than waiting.

All I had of her was the note in my logbook, red ink before pages of stars.

Ten minutes later I ended my day shift early and headed through the sliding doors, balling up my red vest and stuffing it into a pants pocket. I'd taken the name tag off, just in case the sharp stickpin came loose. The last thing I needed was to get jabbed in the scrotum on the walk home—a second time.

Breathing the fresh outdoor air was like surfacing after a deep dive. The air was clear and the sky was blue and cloudless. It was one of those days when you wanted to wad up your work vest and toss it into a trash can to make a point, to show the Man that you didn't need his crap. Of course the Family Friends uniform had cost me twenty bucks, and I'd already replaced it once. So I wasn't exactly in a good financial place for rebellion.

I stood at the crosswalk at Lee Highway and Veitch Street and watched cars rush by, blowing stray plastic bags into the air. I stepped on an empty Styrofoam cup and listened to the pop as it broke into bits. I was looking around for something else to stomp on when the light turned yellow, and while most of the traffic slowed down to a stop, one car accelerated, tearing through the red light like a bat out of hell. I recognized the little Toyota immediately, because I had driven it.

With a grinding of the transmission, Gloria's car slipped into the crowded lanes but was then forced to stop at a different light a little farther up the street. The only way I was able to really identify it was a bumper sticker stuck above the blinking taillight. It read: "My other car is a tank."

The stoplight was red, but it wouldn't stay that way forever, and I knew I had to do something. Now, caution is always important, but there are times in life when action trumps careful contemplation, even if it means putting yourself in mortal danger to sprint across a busy intersection with one shoe untied during a green light.

I took off at full speed, sprinting up the sidewalk pumping my arms like a marathon runner in khakis, and sure, I looked ridiculous, but I made great time. There were a lot of stoplights along Lee Highway, and every time Gloria's car got close to one, I closed my eyes and willed that light to turn red, and I must have been more powerful than I thought, because most of the time it actually worked.

"GLORIA!" I shouted as I flew. "IT'S ME!"

A few blocks ahead she turned left and vanished in a chug of exhaust. I followed with a whoop and shot around the corner, red vest flapping from my pocket like the flaming burst of a jet engine. I buzzed a row of offices, cutting across the psychic's overgrown front lawn and then leaping over the tax attorney's sprinkler. Not even a wall of hedges could stop me, and I exploded through them, sending dried thorns flying like shrapnel. At one point I even flattened a mailbox, but I recovered. The mailbox, however, did not. I sprinted as hard as I could, making a beeline, which is something you can hardly ever do in life.

I had to talk to her again. I couldn't just let her slip away. Not now.

Hitting the street once more, I saw Gloria a block ahead of me, just as she sputtered through a remaining stop sign and into her long black driveway. I gasped, slowed to a walk, and then watched her slowly make her way from the car to the front door. Even when she was the size of my thumb, she looked absolutely breathtaking. A moment later she was inside.

That's when I vomited on a manhole cover.

I wasn't sick, just winded, although I did have a pretty bad scratch on my right arm that was bleeding. I took out my Family Friends vest and tied it tightly around the wound. I really wanted to tear off a strip of cloth with my teeth to make a bandage, like they do in the movies, but I didn't want to have to pay Mr. Pastore another twenty bucks. The wounds were worth it, because I'd seen the chance and I'd taken it. No regrets.

Standing at the low wall that surrounded Gloria's house, I faced a conundrum: I couldn't just walk up to her front door and knock, the classic "I was just in the neighborhood" routine, because I wasn't. There was a flash of movement behind the second-floor curtains, and as I thought back to that moment when the two of us had stood in her sunny bedroom, an idea came to me, triggered by my memory of the sun pouring through her windows. Like Gloria, the plan was a thing of beauty.

It was also completely crazy; but if there was ever a time for insanity, this was it. I had to talk to Gloria. That was the only thing going through my mind. When Superman saves the world, he doesn't question the methods, he just does what needs to be done. Sometimes you needed to leap a tall building in a single bound to get to the girl. Other times you needed to commit a little breaking and entering.

Reaching for my hip pocket, I took out my logbook. Opening it to a page empty of notes or ephemerides, I jotted down a message, tore it out, jotted down a different one, and after three more tries ended up with this:

I followed you home.
—Charlie Wyatt

It was short but sweet, to the point, even courteous. Balling up the paper around a small rock I found in the storm drain, I stepped over the landscaping onto the front lawn, knowing I'd need to get a good running start if I planned to get the note all the way to the second-floor window. The wind was going to be an issue, as it had been storming all week and the gales were so strong they could sometimes pluck the glasses right off your face. That reminded me, and I took out my specs and secured them to my face, squinting into the sun.

After adjusting my balance once, twice, and one final time,

I backed up a step, rocked on a heel, and then went into the windup.

Almost as soon as the note left my fingers, a gust of wind snatched it and hurled it high into the sky. The small stone dropped ineffectively back to the green grass like a meteorite, while the remaining ball of paper floated in an updraft and ended up landing in a rain gutter overlooking a small shed with a weather vane on top.

I didn't know what to do. It seemed like every time I tried to do anything, it backfired. That's how I felt standing on Gloria's front lawn: as if I was always one step away from where I wanted to be. One step forward, forty steps back, and standing on a patch of wet mulch that actually might have been dog poop.

So I faced a new conundrum: I now had to rescue and then deliver my note.

Gloria's house was pretty unscalable. There weren't any trellises or anything, which never seemed to be part of the architecture when you really needed them to be—balconies, either. If you went by *Romeo and Juliet*, you expected those things to be everywhere, but I guess Shakespeare was just making stuff up as he went.

Discouraged, I watched a squirrel scurry across the lawn and up the vinyl siding of a little prefab garden shed that stood close to the house, and then hop onto the overhead power line. That's when I figured out what to do, and I would have hugged that fuzzy little rodent if I hadn't been deathly afraid of rabies.

Scaling the shed was the easy part—there was a pretty deep windowsill—but the gap between the building and the greater house presented a nice challenge—not to say I wasn't up to it, but it required more thought than the usual problem. After turning countless ideas over in my head, weighing my options carefully, and considering all the angles, I decided that my best course of action was to run real fast and jump as far as I could.

That worked about as well as anyone could expect.

Roofs are actually much steeper than they appear from twenty feet down on the ground, and you can only really understand this when you're dangling from the edge of one. After struggling for a minute or two, I began to gradually grope my way up the smooth slate shingles of the incline. I ignored my fear of heights and ascended, although it might have been good if I had stayed slightly terrified, because what I was doing would most likely lead to a shattered spine. Instead of worrying about it, I chose to focus on the task at hand: the climbing.

The phone began to ring quietly in my pants, and even though I shouldn't have, I took one hand off the roof to dig around in my pocket to retrieve it.

"Hello?" I said, answering.

"This is Paul Edison calling for Paul Edison," said Edison.

I shook my head. "I really have to change the ID on this phone. What's up?"

"Is everything okay? You sound winded."

"No. Yeah. Well, I'm on a roof."

"The roof of the drugstore?"

"No, that girl's roof," I said. "I jumped off her garden shed and now I'm holding on to her satellite dish."

"And why are you doing that?"

"I threw a note at her window, but it blew into the gutter."

"I see," he said, thinking. "So I guess now isn't a good time to stop over and get my DVD of *Safety Last!*? I want it for art reference."

"Well, I'm not there," I said, rubbing sweat off my forehead with a sleeve.

"Right," he said, pausing. "You're on the roof."

"Right," I said.

"Didn't I tell you to keep your feet on the ground?" he asked.

"Have I ever been good at listening?" I replied.

His silence was answer enough. "Okay," he said at last, "well, I really don't want to distract you, so I'm going to go now. You, um, hang in there, Charlie."

"Sure thing," I said.

"Call me later, if you're alive."

"Later." And then I turned off the phone with my chin.

I lay there for a while, maybe ten minutes, unsure of what to do. Finally, when I was starting to get bored, and pretty tired, the whole house shuddered as someone slammed a door just below me. I tensed, pulling myself higher up the base of the TV dish, which gave off a creepy hum and was no doubt giving me some obscure form of cancer. At last I reached a skylight, a gray metal frame that peered down through a long shaft into the second floor of the house.

And, of course, it looked down into her bedroom.

Gloria sat at her desk, hunched, staring down at a framed picture she held in both hands. I vaguely remembered the photo. It had sat between the pencil holders and the lamp, a silver rectangle with two faces staring out of it—hers and a boy's. He'd been handsome—I'd caught that. At least better-looking than me, and tanner, and fitter, meaning he had biceps bigger than my head.

The two of us remained unmoving for several minutes.

Something strange happens when you watch the girl you like staring dreamily at a picture of a cute dude with a shaved head and a tight shirt that makes him look like some sort of military superstud. Maybe describing it as a "feeling" isn't very accurate, because when you see this happen, as you're lying there with your sock in the gutter and a cell phone in your teeth, you can't *feel* much of anything.

If not for my general dislike of excruciating pain, I would have let go of the shingles and fallen off that roof, letting myself meet my doom on her driveway. Maybe then Gloria would really notice me, maybe then she'd want to be with me instead of with her dashing beau, with his symmetrical smile and Mediterranean features, a guy she was no doubt madly in love with but who didn't understand how good he really had it. I bet that every time she ran into me, it probably made her miss that guy even more.

I tried to stay quiet and not spy on her until she left the room again. And eventually, she did. It couldn't happen fast enough. All I wanted was to get down off that gutter and go home. Anything was better than where I was.

On her way back out to the car, Gloria lingered on the blacktop for a minute, arms crossed over her chest, and she stared fixedly at the ground instead of up into the open summer sky. I watched from my perch, unseen. Even though I wasn't the person she wanted to be with, I felt bad for her, because she seemed pretty upset that her boyfriend wasn't there.

If I had someone who loved me, I'd probably miss them that much, too.

MAGNET

"SORRY IT TOOK ME SO LONG," I SAID, HURRYING THROUGH THE crowd.

"No worries," said Maggie. "We've been having a nice time." She bugged out her eyes when Mom wasn't looking, acting as if she were being strangled. Nice to know their relationship hadn't changed in half an hour.

The two of them stood beside a flower stall and inspected a pot of morning glories. Shoppers clogged the sidewalks. It was a beautiful day outside, and Georgetown was near critical mass. Cars hardly moved in the jammed intersections. The outdoor seating at every restaurant was full, and lines curled out the front doors. Far away on the river, the shouts of a crew boat captain could be heard. It was louder than the traffic.

"What did you go home for?" asked Maggie, paying the florist.

"Nothing," I said.

"So your journal, then?" she said with a smile.

"No comment."

"What are we talking about now?" asked Mom, turning around. Had she even noticed I'd been gone? Ironic, since she was the reason I'd needed to get my journal in the first place. I didn't feel comfortable without it. Not around her.

"Shopping," I said. "What else?"

"Your sister found a dress she liked," said Mom.

"Correction," said Maggie. "Mom found a dress she *wished* I liked."

"Well, at least it covers you," said Mom.

"Problem number one," said Maggie, raising a finger.

For lunch, we found a bench alongside the old towpath of the C&O Canal, which was now a jogging trail. It was one of the more peaceful areas of Washington DC. The small patch of grass seemed surprisingly tucked away and private, no matter how many times you saw it. It stretched from M Street to the grungy stones of the canal wall. With every step toward the water, the honk of traffic faded behind you more. It was the closest thing to paradise on the Potomac.

(Urban legend has it that one of JFK's lovers was shot on this very towpath. I couldn't imagine a more relaxing place to get murdered.)

We ate sandwiches we bought at a bakery around the corner. We shared a single waxed paper bag and passed a bottle of water among the three of us. The rest of the world seemed miles away. College boys jogged past our bench, shirtless and sweaty. Each one straightened up when he saw Maggie. I'm surprised more of them didn't faint.

As I finished, Maggie and Mom got up. They walked over to a nearby can to toss the trash. When they did, I took out my Freak Folio.

I couldn't go very long without it. It wasn't like losing your keys or misplacing your driver's license. Imagine leaving your heart under your mattress.

Every place I went, I felt like recording what I saw. I even wanted to jot down a few observations from the bakery where we bought lunch. Wherever I went, something nagged at me: a face, a mannerism, a line of dialogue. All of it had potential.

At the bakery, a man had been sitting alone at an outdoor table. He scribbled endlessly on a series of napkins. His beard was huge and tangled. It was tucked into the collar of his grubby white T-shirt. On my way out the door, he held up one of his small paper squares for me to read. "I just want attention" was all it said. It was terrifying, and utterly heartbreaking.

I wrote:

Found insanity today
in a coffee shop
in Georgetown
or maybe it was loneliness.
His old man's eyes wild,
his hands long and slender as chopsticks,
a cigarette burning itself to death
between his yellowed fingers,
waiting to find someone, anyone, me—
a shut door with too many locks.
"I just want attention."
That was all.
The conversation began and ended abruptly.
But so do so many things.
Sparks with a stranger,
cars at red lights,
young lives on battlefields.

I looked up for a second, only to see Maggie head up the hill toward M Street. It wasn't an encouraging sight. Especially since my mother was walking back in my direction *by herself.*

Our eyes met. I looked away quickly.

"Your sister wanted to visit the comic-book shop," said my mother.

"Shocker," I said.

She placed a hand on the seat back. "What are you writing?"

"Nothing."

With a sigh, Mom sat down next to me on the bench. Neither of us spoke. It was as close to a comfortable silence as we could hope for.

The wind blew her silk scarf. It fluttered out over the grass like a flag. Laughing innocently, she snagged it from the air. Then she smiled at me, raising her eyebrows. This was a look I remembered from when I was a kid, when she'd been fun.

There'd been a time when I loved helping my mother. We would prepare for her parties together. She would hold the stepladder as I fetched the china from the highest shelf. It meant something that she chose me. It had been my special job to hold her most fragile pieces, the plates her own mother had given her. Even then I marveled at how clean she kept the top of that cupboard. Even up where no one ever had a reason to see. She made sure it was spotless.

I turned to look at Mom now. Her profile seemed looser than I'd expected, older. The makeup couldn't hide it. Not out in the light of day.

"Mom," I said, eyes back on the toes of my boots, "do I act, I don't know, mean, sometimes?"

"Do you act mean?" she asked.

I rotated the wet water bottle on my kneecap. It left a perfect damp circle on the denim. "Do I push people away? Do I push *you* away?"

It was like I'd told her I was running off to join a terrorist cell. She had a look of pure horror. "Where would you get an idea like that?"

"I have my sources," I said.

She put one of her hands on top of mine. It felt cold, wrinkled. "I would never tell anyone that you push people away."

"But do I?"

"No one says that about you," she said.

I pulled away, furious that she wasn't answering my question. Would she ever just listen to me? "But is it *true*?"

"Honey, you can't ever push away those who love you," she said, smiling as if I were completely insane for even asking.

I thought about what Maggie had told me. How she felt like I hated people for being happy. But it wasn't joy that made me angry. It was something else. It was acting like nothing was wrong. Like nothing had happened. Like you could just go on your merry way and everything would work out fine.

Mom smiled sweetly at me, seemingly A-okay. Frustrated, I searched my surroundings for proof that I wasn't nuts. That everything *wasn't* fine. There wasn't much to go on. I held the crust of a sandwich in my hand. Chocolate covered my fingertips. A piece of wax paper was stuck to my shoe. A runner passed and flashed his smile. The Potomac smelled like fish and trash, not at all as I'd romanticized.

Then all of it—everything in the whole wide world— seemed really stupid. What did any of it matter? I didn't need to find proof of why life sucked. We'd already had enough evidence dumped on us. For a year we'd been buried by it. It was called death.

"You don't seem to care," I blurted.

"I don't seem to care about what?" Mom asked, surprised, as if we hadn't been in the middle of a conversation.

Lightness filled my head. As it did, my nose began to run. "You know what I'm talking about," I said. "It was over so fast. You were sad, and then just as suddenly you weren't anymore." I was crying now. Just like that. Never knew I could do it so quickly.

"Are you referring to what I think you're referring to?" she said. It sounded so businesslike, as if I were a client.

I threw my hands into the air. "*Faris*, Mom, your son!"

Her face went blank, like a dirty window wiped clean. "Yes," she said, "Faris." It was breathless. Not a name, only a hollow, ghostly sound.

Snot oozed down my lip. "He died," I said, "and we had the funeral and everyone was here, and then it was like it had never happened. But it *did* happen. You can't act like everything is the way it used to be, because it's not. It's not!"

She leaned close again and tried to crush my hands in hers. But I knocked them away. "I never stop thinking about your brother," she said. "Not for one second."

"You could have fooled me," I sobbed.

Hearing that, my mother began to shut down.

It was a process I'd witnessed hundreds of times before. One second she was there on the bench with her stylish sunglasses and her one-hundred-and-fifty-dollar hairdo. The next, I was a lunch date of one. "I don't want to talk about this anymore," she said. She even turned slightly to one side to make the point, her back to my sobbing face.

"Well, we need to talk about it sometime," I said, "because I don't know if I can ever be as fine with it as you are, Mom."

"I am not '*fine with it*,' Gloria," she said coldly.

That did it. I'd almost said everything I'd wanted to say on the issue. Almost. I glared hard at my mother and wiped away tears with the heel of my hand. "Sometimes it feels like I'm the only one who grieves in this family," I finished.

This time I did not look away. I wanted her to know I meant it.

Trembling, my mother reached out and took her purse from where it sat at our feet. She stood up, tall, beautiful, not a hair out of place. Then, slipping the strap over one shoulder, she lifted her chin enough to say "I grieve" in a small, wounded voice. "Just not as dramatically as you do."

Then she walked away along the river.

FREAK

"GLORIA," I SAID BREATHLESSLY, LIKE ANY GIRL WOULD PROBABLY want her name spoken. It was like a last gasp before kicking the bucket.

I sat on a stool behind the cash register, surrounded by boxes of electric razors and children's DVDs, and Gloria stood just beyond the shoplifting scanners wearing a dress of daisies and white, her small red umbrella draining onto our big black welcome mats. She'd walked out of the rain like a paling hallucination, and for a second I wondered if one of the other guys had turned over a tub of chemicals in the photo lab and I was high, but I didn't smell anything, so I was pretty sure I was safe.

Gloria was real. She was enchanting. All I wanted to do was look and keep looking.

She'd caught me mid word-bubble, sucking an M&M and reading *Action Comics* number 867, at just the moment when Superman rescues the bottled city of Kandor from his old enemy Brainiac. Amid the other clutter on the counter sat my black logbook and a copy of *Foundations of Modern Cosmology*, which had been specified as required reading for my trip next month. It was sort of a snore.

To say that concentrating on my studies had been difficult would be an incredible understatement. Nothing held my attention anymore, not even the possible comet I'd been tracking since April. All I could think about was Gloria, and how when I left town in the beginning of August, I'd be leaving her, too, just as I was starting to feel like we were reaching each other, like two stray signals broadcast across the great vastness of space.

After shaking her umbrella, Gloria folded it as the automatic doors slid shut behind her. Then she smoothed the front of her dress and flipped her hair. Shiny amber earrings caught the drugstore light. I stared. It was like a scene in some classic romance film—Phil Collins on the overhead speakers, thunder shaking the ground under our feet, a giant novelty sausage with the slogan "It's Grilling Time!" strung above our heads on an oversize plastic fork.

We were alone. The store was empty due to the storm, and I hadn't seen a soul since seven o'clock when I'd taken over Mr. Pastore's night shift. Gloria's wet footprints were the only ones drying on the speckled gray tile.

"Wow," I said, checking out the fanciness of her dress. "Did you win something?"

"Hi, Charlie," she said, smiling. "No." A small paper shopping bag hung from around one of her wrists.

"You look nice," I added.

She blushed. "Thanks."

I lit up inside.

It was difficult to contain my excitement as I waited for her next move, which didn't happen right away. Even she didn't seem to know what she was doing. No matter what she had in mind, I was so glad to see her.

The girl in front of me was a bit different from the one I was used to. For a moment I entertained the possibility that perhaps Gloria had a twin sister, and that the two of them had been playing a trick on me this whole time, but that seemed pretty unlikely. Her hair was incredibly cute, playful even, and I could finally see her big brown eyes without having them vanish every few seconds under a dyed black curtain. Instead of big combat boots or platforms, she wore a pair of shiny flat shoes that were the color of butterscotch and revealed the truly itty-bitty size of her feet. I didn't know how she kept her balance with feet so small. The dress was the clincher, because it was unlike anything she'd ever worn before, and it suited her in a way I couldn't have imagined at first. It evolved her.

"How have you been?" she asked at last, stepping closer, butterscotch shoes making squeaks on the wet floor.

"Why are you dressed up?" I asked, having already blanked on the question she'd just asked me. I couldn't help it. I couldn't take my eyes off her.

She stopped and took a deep breath. "My mom has this awards event for her foundation, and every year we have to dress up just to make her happy. Otherwise she gets on our cases. Of course, I don't always want to dress up like I'm going to the ball just because she tells me to."

After the last word spilled out, she added, "But I love this dress." She smoothed the front of the fabric again, a new nervous habit. "I got it today and just . . . wanted to wear it somewhere."

Then, from out of nowhere, she said, "I'm sorry."

"Why are you sorry?"

"You called and I never called you back," she said. "It's rude."

I hung my head, remembering. "Don't be sorry," I said.

Gloria leaned on the counter, not looking at me really but off into the blistering fluorescence of the empty aisles. "Our family's been going through some stuff," she said. "And I've been a little out of it." Then she glanced at me and noticed the button I'd recently added to my work vest. It made her chuckle. "Maybe I should have come and found you sooner."

The button said ASK ME ABOUT WHAT FAMILY FRIENDS CAN DO FOR YOU. Its yellow smiley face made me remember how happy I'd been that afternoon when I'd chased Gloria home. It also reminded me how sad I'd felt after getting trapped on her roof, getting pooped on by a bird, and then finding out that there was some other guy in her life, a guy with skin that glinted brown in the sun like a penny.

"I probably shouldn't have called you," I said.

But I didn't stop there—when I'd dangled shoeless from her satellite dish—but went all the way back to the beginning when we'd first met. "And I probably shouldn't have talked to you that day in DC, either. That was *not* cool." Bobbing my head, I tried to focus on customer service and not making a fool out of myself. "I have the tendency to sort of talk, like, just for me, and not really think about how things might sound to other people. Not that I needed to tell you." I exhaled heavily, snatching an M&M from my open bag. "I guess I just felt like you and I had a connection."

Telling this to Gloria's face, as she stood there wearing a sundress on a rainy day, was probably the most embarrassing thing I'd ever done in my whole life. But I wanted to be myself. I had to.

She waited for me to finish and then spoke. "Is that why you threw that note up on my roof?"

The M&M I was sucking on got stuck in my throat, and I raised a finger, so she knew to give me a moment. Then I hacked, inhaled sharply, coughed once, and proceeded to spit the blue candy into my palm, where it slowly turned my skin brown. "Possibly," I wheezed.

"It was sitting in our driveway when I got home today," she said. "It was weird. So I knew it was you. Tried for the roof, but didn't count on the wind. Poor Charlie."

"Right," I said. It occurred to me that I had to end the conversation, since she had a boyfriend and all. I didn't want to be a home wrecker, or whatever.

Gloria reached out and touched my shoulder. That didn't help. If I was supposed to be giving her space, it didn't help that she kept getting closer.

"It's okay, Charlie," she said, smiling. "It's fine. It was sweet."

"I'm the *Titanic* of dumb," I said, feeling like a huge jerk. "No, the *Hindenburg* of idiots, exploding into flames. Man overboard!"

"Really, it's okay. Don't get upset."

"I shouldn't have bothered you."

"It's not a big deal."

I thought of the picture of her and the guy that sat on her

dresser. "It is when you have a boyfriend."

She stared at me, perplexed, and then she laughed. "I don't have a boyfriend, Charlie."

I blinked. There were no words.

"Really," she said, seeing my reaction.

Then it all made sense: the meetings, the arguments, the near misses, the poems, and finally, the visit to where I worked, all dressed in her Sunday best. I was being tested. This was some kind of cosmic gauntlet, pushing me to see how far I'd take it. Chile be damned. I was being prepared for something bigger.

"Hang out with me," I blurted, "tonight, at the store." I'd gone from devastation to hope in a heartbeat, like how Edison could crank his car from zero to sixty in less than six seconds. I had to do something.

"I can borrow my friend's PlayStation," I said, growing more agitated. "We can play one of those guitar video games or something, or if there's a TV show you like, we can watch that. I don't care what we do, but we'll have fun."

I stopped thinking of my mom and dad and our dingy little apartment and ALMA and all the responsibilities and plans. I just stopped thinking altogether. "I mean, do you even remember the last time you actually had fun?" I said. "Because I don't remember the last time *I* did."

"Maybe for a few minutes," she said.

I could have hugged her just then, and nothing would have made me happier. I only smiled and imagined it in my head.

"What did you have in mind?" she asked next.

"Wait for one second," I said, grabbing my ratty logbook. I scrawled a note on an empty page and tore it loose and then anchored the paper to the countertop with a can of energy drink. The note read:

Be back in a minute. Please leave the money on the counter. Don't steal. I mean it!

—Charlie Wyatt, Customer Service Associate

And they said I was bad at my job.

I grabbed hold of the ladder and climbed, rung by rung, toward the roof and the sound of the storm, like a thousand feet stomping. Once I reached the platform at the top, I unlocked the small metal door with the key Mr. Pastore had given me on my first day of work. Below me, Gloria waited patiently, her hair still dripping from before. The greasy hinges of the trapdoor screeched, and as I pushed it open, a wave of rain hit us both square in the face. Together, we squeezed up through the hole in the roof.

We huddled under a small awning, a single white bulb casting eerie shadows. The streetlamps of Arlington glowed in every direction, weak and smeary in the gloom, like one of those impressionistic paintings of stars and smog. "It's pretty bad out," I said. "That dress is too nice to drench." I turned to go. "Maybe this isn't a good plan."

Then, taking off her shoes and flinging them aside, Gloria gazed out over the soaked black rooftop. "It's not that bad," she said.

About fifteen feet from the awning stood a small outdoor tent that was meant to give shade on sunny days. It was rainbow striped, part of the "Lawn and Garden" collection, and could be yours for a very reasonable forty dollars, thirty-five dollars with a coupon. I'd put it together on my first day at Family Friends, about seven minutes after receiving my roof key. It was a place I could go to get away from Arnold and angry customers and everyone else who threatened to bring me down. My cheap little shelter stood near one of the roof's enormous industrial air-conditioning units, and its plastic poles bowed in the rain. Underneath its billowing peak sat two rainbow mesh lawn chairs, a white Styrofoam cooler, and a cheap Tasco reflection telescope on a flimsy tripod, all safely tucked out of the downpour. This was my secret lair, my Fortress of Solitude, my hiding place.

"Looks dry enough," said Gloria, referring to the small tent.

"You think?" I said.

"Come on," she said, taking my hand and dragging me out into the weather.

We crossed the cold gravel at a sprint, our free hands over our heads as if that would actually keep us from getting soaked. The air and the rain were warm, and the blowers on the AC units shot the drops sideways into our faces as we passed. I couldn't help but laugh, and Gloria did, too, and with clothes flattened to our skin we reached the cover of the tent, streams of water curling under our chins and hair plastered to our skulls in wet black slicks.

We stood for a second, both of us grinning.

Then she let go of my hand and stepped away from me. "I . . ." she started to say, and then finished with "My brother died."

Wind tore at the tent. Gravel pinged off the metallic blowers and units. I looked down at Gloria's face, which was frozen totally blank.

"Is that a joke?" I asked.

Then she started laughing again. "No. It's not." Then just as quickly back to a straight face. "My brother died last year."

"And he's still dead?" I asked, which I knew was a dumb thing to say. I knew this as soon as I'd said it.

"Yeah," she said, almost as if she couldn't believe it herself. "*Still.*"

I didn't have any satisfying responses for sad news of this magnitude, so I did the next best thing and walked to one of the lawn chairs and offered her a seat. It was dry. It was clean. Its straps would hold her weight. "Please," I said. It was all I could think of to say. And she sat.

I opened the small Styrofoam cooler, the lid of which I'd weighted with another can of energy drink, and pulled out a juice box and handed it to Gloria. She took it without even seeing what it was and began to nurse at the skinny plastic straw, her parted hair hanging down on either side of her face like the heavy, floppy ears of a drenched dog.

"It's nice up here," she said, looking around.

"It's not normally this wet," I said. It was like we were in the middle of a hurricane. I had to lean forward in my chair just to hear her.

"Well, I like it," she said, and then clammed up, feet balanced on a corner of the cooler.

"How did he die?" I asked.

"In Afghanistan," she said. "He was in the military."

"Wow," I said. "That's brave."

"He was," she said quietly, "with everything."

I didn't know what to do next. This was all sort of unfamiliar territory for me, deep conversation, a beautiful girl, the sharing of drinks. It was nothing like how I'd imagined my first date, except for maybe the juice boxes.

"Are you okay?" I asked, because it seemed like an appropriate question.

"This kind of thing happens to everybody," she said. "And I don't understand why I can't get through it. Why I can't get to a place where it doesn't hurt so much." When she talked her voice sounded snotty, so I offered her a sheet of paper towel from a roll I kept in the cooler. "I feel like I can't talk about it or I bring everyone down. Like it's some big secret, like I'm the only one who notices."

I thought about this, about hiding your sadness because you worry it will make those around you feel sad, too. "Everybody has that problem," I told her.

"Not you," she said, toasting me with her fruit punch. "You're like the most positive person in the universe."

I took a deep breath. Again, in the rooftop shadows I could just make out the wet shine of her arms and the whites of her eyes. "Want to know *my* weakness?" I asked.

Her juice box buckled as she drained the last of its contents and began sucking out air. She gave me a look that said she doubted I had a weakness, and if I hadn't already wanted to kiss her, I definitely would have wanted to kiss her then. "Okay," she said.

I opened my mouth. I paused. For once, I didn't have a word backed up on my tongue, waiting like a bullet to fire. "My mom has this disease."

She watched me curiously. "What disease?"

"It's called Huntington's," I said. "It's pretty rare, and . . . it's pretty awful."

She stared at me, her face still giving nothing away. "I'm sorry," she said.

It sounded weird, the way she said "I'm sorry," as if she'd done something. People always said that to be nice, to acknowledge your crummy luck, but I'd come to realize that tragedy wasn't anyone's fault and ended up visiting all of us at one time or another. The "who," "what," "where," "when," and "how" didn't matter. It was the "why" that never made any sense, and it's where all the apologies started.

"I guess I'm sorry, too," I said. "And I'm really scared."

I leaned forward in my chair, elbows on my knees. "With my mom, it's like I'm slowly fading out of existence. Like sometimes she can't hear me, or if she does she barely understands me. You get this feeling, like you can't fight back, you can't change things. All you want is to feel like you can do something. Otherwise," I said, running my hands through my damp hair, "you give up. That's what people do."

Staring down at my interlaced fingers, I thought about Gloria's brother, who I'd never met. One day he'd been there, and the next he hadn't. I couldn't imagine the pain of it, like the car crash that had changed Edison's life in an instant, in one loud boom. That kind of pain was so different from what I'd endured over the last ten years; I'd had nearly a decade to mourn the loss of my mother and move past it, to face all those fears with her right by my side.

I imagined walking into my mom's room the next morning, opening the blinds to let the sunlight in, and finding her bed empty. The world's worst magic trick.

Gloria stripped off a piece of paper towel and pressed it against her cheek, making a dark face-shaped splotch on the quilted pattern. Most of her makeup came off, too, in streaks of color, like she was washing away in the rain. Slowly, she crumpled the whole thing into a squishy ball. "I always picture him in his army gear, which to me was just a lame excuse for jokes. To him they were work clothes. They actually meant something." She tossed the wadded towel into the cooler. "My jokes weren't even funny. Nothing is funny anymore."

"It's all about getting through the day," I said, understanding. "Nothing you do or think seems to ever matter, and over time, if you're not careful, you start to become this person you're not, because your whole life becomes about this one *thing*."

Gloria nodded. "Right," she said, agreeing.

Then, unexpectedly, she reached out and took my hand, turning it over and wrapping her fingers around mine. They warmed me.

MAGNET

HIS HAND WAS SO HOT AND SLICK. FOR A LONG TIME I THOUGHT IT was on the verge of sliding free of my grasp. So I held on. And he held on. And neither of us slipped away.

It was late. We'd watched several neighborhood stores extinguish their lights and close. When I asked Charlie if he wanted to go back downstairs and lock the front doors, he said no. (I think he was as scared to let go of my hand as I was to let go of his.)

Our wrists were bent at unnatural angles, but for some reason it was comfortable. Normally I didn't like touching people. Most of the time I sat counting the seconds until people let go of me. Hugs were timed by breaths. Kisses

193

on the cheek I endured with my eyes shut, jaw clenched tight.

In the past, getting close to someone had always been easy for me. Too easy. I was always so eager to let people in. This applied to anyone I found remotely interesting, to strangers. After Faris, all that changed.

The problem with getting physically close to other people is that you reach a point where you can feel their heartbeat. That's what love is. It's sharing someone else's pulse. When one of those beats suddenly ceases, it's like yours does, too. Why would anyone—*anyone*—ever put themselves through that again? It just didn't make sense.

"I brought you up here because I wanted to show you something," said Charlie, standing up. He lifted my hand and pulled me to my feet. It was as though he were escorting me along a dance floor, instead of perching under a saggy party tent on the rooftop of a strip mall.

"Are you going to use the telescope?" I asked.

He smiled. "No. That Tasco is a piece of junk. Besides, it's too rainy."

"Is that what you normally do up here?" I asked. "*Gaze?*"

"Yeah," he said, and then he did something I'd never seen him do. The kid blushed. Just like some damned grade-school kid with a crush. "Astronomy is sort of what I do."

"That's awesome," I said.

"Is it?" he asked, and he meant it. He didn't know.

"So can you, like, chart my horoscope or something?"

"That's astrology," he said. "They're completely different. Astronomy is scientific study while astrology is more of a symbolic language, superstition. Like, 'Hey, what's your sign?'"

I could have smacked myself. "Oops, I knew that. Really, I did." Then I smiled. "So what is *your* sign?"

"Aries," he said.

"Me too," I said, and we both seemed pleased with the coincidence.

Standing half in the rain again, he hesitated. Then he said, "Just one sec . . ." and pulled his hand away. He disengaged slowly, to get us used to the idea. I didn't like it.

At the bottom of the Styrofoam cooler was a flashlight. No, it was larger than that, a spotlight. The top was as big around as a softball and had a handle, like a gun. It seemed like an odd thing to keep in a cooler. But I knew that if I started asking questions of Charlie now, I'd venture down a road of no return.

He turned on the light with the press of a button. A shaft of dazzling white split the darkness. Then he turned it off. Then he turned it on again. Charlie kept this up—on and off, light and night. It was as if he were trying to keep the beat to a very complicated and unpredictable song.

After a minute or so of this, he turned to me proudly. It took me by surprise. I wondered if I'd missed something.

A small twinkle appeared in the distance, breaking through the drab sheets of rain. It died almost as soon as it had started.

"Did you see that?" I asked, straining my eyes.

"What?" he asked. He hadn't noticed it with his back to the river.

"A light," I said.

"You saw it?" he asked excitedly. Then he spun around and began to flash his spotlight again. He did it smiling, like a kid playing a video game. The trigger made a metal springy noise.

"What is it?" I asked him, trying to see what he saw. "Please tell me you're not looking for UFOs or something."

"I wish," he said, distracted. He kept clicking.

It was as if he were having a silent conversation with someone I couldn't see. Then I realized that this was exactly what was happening.

Somewhere across the Potomac, in the hills of DC, a small spike of ivory light flashed. It blinked twice and then went out.

I grabbed Charlie's arm. "I hope you're not, like, diverting planes by accident."

"No," he said. "It's just Georgetown. That's where she lives."

"Who lives in Georgetown?"

"Gayle," he said. "I don't know her last name."

You couldn't see the stars that night. The clouds were so black that the moon was a suggestion of itself. But as we stood there under the tent, the rain weakening, a constellation appeared. Within a few minutes there were five different spotlights blinking at us. That gravel rooftop became the center of our universe.

"The first time I climbed up here, I just came to track celestial bodies, to mark the stars," said Charlie, "and to be alone, even though I didn't want to be, really. Then one night, after a bad day, I had this idea, and I got a book from the library. It taught Morse code."

Then he pointed toward the darkness of Georgetown. "That's Gayle," he said. "She works in the college library. She got dumped by her fiancé."

He turned to another point of light to his right, the south. "That's Win over there. He's a gay barista, and he hates it, the barista part, I mean."

"You know these people?" I asked. What he was doing floored me. I could barely stand to exchange two words with my own mother. And here was Charlie, talking to lonely hearts with a fancy flashlight. It was his Bat Signal.

"Cynthia, Luz, and Thomas," he said, rotating in a circle, naming the rest of them.

"That's amazing," I said.

I marveled at the skill it must take to hold a conversation

across such vast distances. With people you've never even met, or heard, or even seen. In Morse code! Even more, though, I was impressed with Charlie's willingness to reach out.

"You know," he said, watching me, "sometimes it helps to know that there are other people out there, and that feeling different, or alone, doesn't make you that way."

Charlie was right. As we stood together in the drizzle, I wanted to know him better—desperately.

So I stepped forward, and I kissed him.

His face was turned sideways when I did it, and my movement took him by surprise. He flinched as though I'd come at him with a knife. But then he froze. And it was perfect. For those few seconds I wasn't alone, and he wasn't different. Our faces burned hot in the mist and they touched. Up that close, I saw a scar that arced across his left temple, like a shooting star.

Then it was over. He stepped back. Neither of us knew what to say.

Suddenly I remembered what I'd brought with me in my Macy's shopping bag. A gift was a good way to communicate without needing to talk.

All I wanted to do was kiss him again, to feel his cheek against mine one more time. Charlie had done more for me in that half hour than anyone had been able to do in a year. I felt close to someone again. (I'd almost forgotten what that felt like.) But I was scared, too.

Nervous, I walked over to my chair, where I'd set the paper sack under the saggy rainbow straps. "I brought you something," I said. "You may not need it, or want it." I took out the leather journal, the one I'd bought earlier that day. It was tied with a red ribbon.

"What's that?"

"It's nothing as poetic as a Morse-code light show," I said. I suddenly felt really cheap, silly.

Giving him such a present only revealed my shallowness. What he'd done for me had been spectacular. It was moving. What I'd done for him was spend a few dollars. Not even that many. Charlie was a better person than me. Eventually he would figure that out.

"It's a journal," he said, hurrying over. "It's super fancy."

"I know how much you like the clearance stuff," I said, shrugging.

He took it and then spent a long time staring at the leather. "You got my note, right?" I said. "You needed a new notebook." He kept staring. I was starting to feel uncomfortable, like I'd crossed some kind of line. (Was there a line with Charlie?)

Slowly, he thumbed through the first stiff pages. "Thank you," he said quietly, petting the fake leather. "No one's ever given me a gift for no reason."

"I wrote in this one, too," I said, "something longer this time."

Holding the journal delicately, he read what I'd written on the inside cover.

When he finished, he looked up. His eyes were wide. The scar by his temple had turned bright white against his reddening skin. "I don't know when it happened," he said quietly, "but you've become really special to me."

He didn't expect me to say the same, even though we both knew it was true.

"I know I say a lot," he went on, "but I mean that."

Face in shadow, he stepped toward me. To do what, I didn't know—to kiss me again, to hug me, to shake my hand—maybe all of them. I never found out. Because that's when I left, when I took one last look at him standing there with the journal against his heart, and ran.

I thought about the inscription. With every step across the gravel, I remembered, with every rung of the ladder and every slippery click across the pharmacy floor. They were words I meant but regretted ever putting down in writing.

I meant them because they were true. I regretted them for that very same reason:

I build conversations in my clattering brain
when no one else is here to work the details.
People live and die between my ears.

But you spit it all out—
splintered wood and broken nail heads,
frantically building out into the world.

And suddenly there is a bridge
where before all that spanned the divide
was silence.

FREAK

SEEING GLORIA INSPIRED ME. IT ALWAYS DID. SHE'D LOOKED SO divine in her white and yellow dress and little elf hairdo, small doll shoes with those small doll feet squeezed into them, so beautiful that I had trouble drifting off to sleep. My insomnia had nothing to do with the fact that she'd left me sitting all by my lonesome in the drizzle of the rooftop. I knew that whatever had driven her away had been important, an emergency. She never would have left me like that otherwise.

The next day, I woke up around seven and showered, shaved, and tapped some of the cologne my dad had given me for my last birthday into the palms of my hands. I'd never used cologne before because it made my skin turn red and bumpy and my eyes itch, so I didn't know exactly how to dab it on or where, but after some intense thought, I placed a small drop behind each ear and called it a day.

Instantly, I felt transformed. The skinny teenage Charlie Wyatt was gone, and in his place stood a gnarled, leathery, world-weary dude, reeking of strength and alcohol. I was ready to face the world. There was only one thing left to do, and that was finish the transformation from Charlie Wyatt, mild-mannered boy astronomer, to Kal-El, last son of Krypton—or Superman, as he's known in traditional circles.

After dressing, I sat on the edge of my bed for a minute or two and listened to the hiss of the baby monitor I kept on my dresser. Dad and I both had them in our rooms, in case Mom needed anything or had an accident in the middle of the night. The illuminated red bar jumped as she coughed once and drew out a wheeze, and then she fell silent, repositioning. The world sounded so far away through that crackly speaker. Even though Mom was just a hallway away, it sounded as though she were broadcasting from across the galaxy, from some desolate moon.

On the bedside table next to my good telescope lay the new leather journal, its spine still rigid. It was a gift, for me. I smiled, unable to get Gloria out of my head—in that outfit, its flowery trim cutting through the darkness like a candle you wanted to put your hand over to keep safe.

Thinking about how she'd braved the rain to reveal to me the side of her that was the most fragile, to tell me about her brother, I knew I needed to reciprocate, to show courage, too. But that meant giving up the suit.

Now, I knew it was kind of crazy to wear a costume around every day under your clothes. And I wasn't nuts. Everyone in the world gets by with a little help. In *Superman*, he has powers, like superspeed, flight, or heat vision; but in reality we make do without the drama, and we clutch for our morning cappuccino or play online games with our friends or grow a goatee to hide the big mole on our chin. Some people can't walk, so they buy fast cars. Others still fantasize about high school because that's when they were big football stars and the envy of everyone. We do what we can to feel good, to feel powerful, but mostly to feel like we've got some tiny influence on our own lives.

Heroes like Superman work to change the world. Humans, well, we do our best just to keep our own lives from falling apart.

I wanted to stand up under my own strength again . . . but maybe I wasn't ready yet. After all, I'd worn the costume for eight months, and that wasn't anything to sneeze at. So the tights stayed on, although to be totally honest, they were getting a little snug in the crotch.

Taking the journal with me, I went to the kitchen and

checked the time on the microwave. It was nearly nine o'clock. I was late. With a shout good-bye, I rushed to the elevator, traveled down to the lobby, and then sprinted down Soleil Day's semicircular drive to the sidewalk leading south. I jogged along the road toward the courthouse, glimpsing the colored lights of Arlington through the Potomac fog. I kept thinking of how the journal would replace my beat-up old logbook and hold a place of honor amid my luggage for the Chile trip. There'd be my toothbrush, my underwear, and Gloria's gift—the essentials.

I reached the Grind House in between morning rushes and found a stool at the long counter near the front of the store where I could see the streets and the people approaching from all over, and I waited for him. I opened my journal and set the pen down in the binding. The expanse of white pages stared back at me, all mine.

"If it isn't the chimney sweep," said Edison, rolling through the front door. "Cling to any roofs lately?"

"Dude, you are never going to believe what I have to tell you," I said, preparing him for the tales of my most recent adventures.

"How come I never like it when you say that?" he said with a wink.

"Imagine this," I said, hands flailing. "It's a dark and stormy night."

"Hold that thought," he said, wheeling past me to where the barista was taking orders. "Coffee is required."

He was making me wait on purpose, as torture, because he knew I couldn't hold on to gossip for very long before exploding.

When he finally returned, I was about ready to get up and start doing jumping jacks, I was so tense. He very deliberately added sugar to his coffee, stirred, more sugar, stirred. "Okay, go," he said once he was settled, his face split with a wicked grin.

So I told him about my harrowing afternoon on Gloria's roof, and about the heartbreak I suffered at the discovery that she had a boyfriend, but then ended with the triumphant tale of our encounter on the Family Friends roof, and how wonderfully she fit into a dress. Through the whole story, he grinned with cheer and anticipation, like a kid watching someone scoop him an ice-cream cone. I ended with the kiss, which I explained couldn't have lasted for more than maybe three seconds, but how it felt like one hundred times that. When I finished, he actually leaned over and hugged me— the man kind of hug, which is all about shoulders and the slapping of backs.

"Charlie," he said, "I am impressed, truly. I could have sworn this entire thing was going to end in disaster. And actually"—and he took a drink—"I'm amazed you weren't discouraged by her initial rejection."

"Do I usually get discouraged?" I asked.

He took his time answering, blowing in the hole of his drink's plastic lid. "It depends," he said. "When you're flying, you soar, man. But when you choose to join humanity and things don't work out, well, you crash hard. Like a meteor or something." He sipped, gaze on the tabletop instead of on me.

"Meteors don't hit the Earth," I corrected him. "Those are meteorites."

"Meteorites, whatever," he said. "The point is that you don't mess around."

"I'm not *that* bad," I said.

"Remember your dad's heart attack?" he asked.

"What would you expect?" I said, getting angry. I didn't want to sit there on a perfect morning thinking about the past, dwelling on tragedy. Things were looking up.

"Anyone would be upset, Charlie," he said. "But you locked yourself in a gas station bathroom."

"I didn't know what to do."

"You attacked the station attendant!"

I slammed shut the journal. "Listen!" I said. "Today is a good day, one of the best, so why are you deliberately trying to ruin it? I thought you were my friend."

"I am your friend, your *best* friend," he said, lowering his voice. "It's just Charlie Wyatt physics. You're always so much higher than the rest of us, and the higher you fly, the farther you have to fall." He shrugged and swirled his coffee around in the cup. "I just worry about you. You're like my brother, only crazy and oblivious and much too tall."

"You too," I said. A wave of affection swept over me, and I suddenly felt like returning his embrace and wrapping my arms around Edison's skinny little waist. "I don't know what I'm going to do without you."

"Tell me about it," he said. "Why do you think I'm always trying to keep you on the straight and narrow? I just want to deliver you to the airport on the morning of August second, alive, sane, and ready to discover some seriously cosmic shit."

"And you will," I said, but for some reason, I wasn't entirely convinced of my own words.

"I understand this girl is cool, Charlie, but this internship is big, and you've been planning for it since the winter. It's no time to go all *Charlie*."

"I won't."

"We'll see," he said, picking up on what I'd just sensed: doubt. "You've still got some work to do before Chile. It's only about three weeks away."

"I'll be fine," I said.

He paused, staring probingly at me. "How long have you worn that costume now?" he asked. "It's been what, like, six months?"

I didn't look at him. "About eight," I answered.

"You can't hide in that forever, man."

"I'm not hiding."

"It doesn't do anything."

"I know!" I slammed a fist down on the counter.

Didn't he understand that I wanted a normal life more than anything? When I left the Grind House, I would have to go home and feed Mom, and then I'd have to clean the house and make her breakfast for the next morning, and after that, instead of sitting down to zone out in front of the TV or maybe going to a comic shop to browse, I would sit by the baby monitor and look up at the sky, hoping to catch a glimpse of a collection of rock, dust, ice, and gases, because if something happened to Mom I'd need to be there, because without me, everything would come apart.

To do all that, I needed to believe that I could—me, Charlie Wyatt.

"You okay?" asked Edison, watching me closely.

"Fine," I said.

"You sure?" he asked.

"You know, life is tough for some of us," I said without thinking.

Edison stared at the coffee cup in front of him, which had stopped steaming and gone cold. Then he raised his wheelchair up on the back wheels and dropped it back down again with a clank. "Right," he said grumpily, "and some of us are just *lucky*."

I reached out and touched his arm. "I'm sorry."

"Shit isn't always about you, Charlie," he grumbled.

"It isn't," I said.

"From the moment we met, I knew you were different," he said, fingering a tire tread. "Hell, we hadn't even known each other that long when I had the accident. But there you were, at the hospital more than my parents were."

"I remember," I said.

He took deep breaths as he talked, calm. It was as if I didn't even need to be there. "I've thought about this, and I think we're actually a lot alike."

"Yeah?"

"Yeah. We've both had the rugs pulled out from under us, and we've spent a long time trying to get back on our feet." Then he glanced down at his shoes, propped as they were on the little footrests. "In a manner of speaking."

"Paul," I said, insisting. I put my hand on his arm. "I'm sorry, man."

At last he turned to me, eyes everywhere but on my face. "I know," he said. "I just don't want you to get hurt. You've finally found stability, and it scares me when you veer from it. You know what they say? In the absence of order, there's chaos."

I smiled at him, but he didn't seem reassured. Maybe I needed to take the costume off sooner than I'd anticipated.

My alter ego was getting lost. I'd used my secret identity for so long that I didn't remember who I was without it.

Luckily my best friend did.

I walked into the apartment a little after ten. Dad had been on the job for almost three hours and was waiting for me to get home before going down to the seventh floor to poke around in someone's heat register. He raised his arm to high-five me as we passed in the entryway, but I strolled right by him, head down and lost in what Edison had said.

Needing guidance, I opened Mom's bedroom door and found it filled with darkness. I raised the shades as far as they could go and cracked the window to let in a cool breeze and then went to her bedside.

We sat together in silence and took in the morning sounds: the creaking of the house as it settled, the gurgle of Dad's second pot of coffee switching on at ten thirty, a squirrel that kept scrabbling around in the branches outside the window a few floors down. She looked particularly pale that morning, as if she'd shed a layer of skin during the night like a snake. The veins in her face seemed darker, the hairs clinging to her scalp thinner and whiter. More than once I wondered if she was simply faking the whole thing, if it was an elaborate hoax to find out how the rest of us really acted, because at this point we were often our true selves in front of Mom. That's because sometimes we forgot she was even there. That's how little she spoke, how precious her words were.

Resting against one of her pillows, I stroked her warm forehead, unable to keep from smiling as I remembered how she'd done the same for me on the nights when I'd woken up with a cough. I took care of myself now.

"Hey, Mom," I said, and gently kissed her on the cheek. You could feel the bone under there, a hard edge in what was once so soft.

I didn't expect an answer right away, or if one came I knew it might not have anything to do with the question.

And I talked to her like I always did, told her about what Edison had said, and how Arnold and Lawrence at work were huge slackers who didn't know a thing about customer service, unless customer service meant smoking cigarettes out behind the Dumpsters with a couple of girls who worked the meat station at the make-your-own-burrito place two blocks over. Then I took her hand and held it.

"Remember Gloria?" I asked. I didn't wait for a reply. "She came to the store last night, Mom."

"Gloria?"

"Yeah. She came to the store. She was wearing the prettiest dress."

"The store?"

"You know, where I work."

"The store."

"Gloria came to see me there."

"Gloria."

"Yeah, and I really like her, Mom."

"Gloria?"

I said it again, to hear myself. "I really like her."

I held my tongue for a second but then continued. "And part of me wonders if I should cancel the South America trip, ask if I can go in the spring, or next summer. There's just something gnawing at me, a feeling. Things are changing, and I'm afraid that if I don't act right now, my chance with Gloria will be gone."

Describing our relationship that way made me think of comets, of Halley, Biela, and Olbers. Their elliptical orbits cause them to streak by in a flash and disappear, not to return for decades, even centuries. And those orbits were considered short. Could I wait a century for another shot with someone like Gloria?

I squeezed Mom's hand. "You know the small solar body I've been following? The object I think is a comet?"

No reply.

"I'm going to name it for you." This made me smile, like it always did. "Comet Dorothy. The typical nomenclature has discoveries being named after the observer who discovers it, but I figured it was my comet, my call."

Mom's eyes remained averted and glassy. She seemed to be watching the way the sunlight played along the windowsill through the blinds, small slits of orange. Nothing moved but the rise and fall of her chest under the sheet.

I sat, and I waited, for anything, for that wonderful "Charlie" like the sighing of an accordion. Whatever word she managed, I expected to hold it inside like a deep breath.

But nothing came.

"Mom?" I said, pulling at the skin over her knuckles. My heart felt leaden in my chest, a stone, not even beating. "Mom?"

A cry welled up inside me, one I'd been working on for years. She was gone!

"What?" she said suddenly.

I blinked and then released the air trapped in my chest. "Oh, God," I murmured.

Her gaze snapped from the windowsill to my face. "What the fuck do you want?"

"Nothing," I said, slightly taken aback by the profanity.

"Then get me a cigarette," she snapped.

I wasn't sure whether to stand up or not, whether she was playing some sort of game, acting; but it'd never been like her to swear, and if she had, she certainly hadn't done it in front of me. "You haven't smoked in, like, six years," I reminded her.

"Did I ask for a fucking history lesson?"

"No, I just—"

"Then do it, asshole."

Normally I like to think of myself as someone who gets things done, as a man of action, but after hearing those venomous words drip from my mother's lips, I couldn't move a muscle. I sat by the bed staring into her face, gaunt and foreign as it was. Her eyes were bloodshot, the corners tinged with scarlet.

"Mom, I—"

Then she slapped me.

ARIES
3/21–4/19

You have a lot to offer others. If you slip up a little today, don't worry too much.

MAGNET

"CAN I COME IN?" THE DOOR HANDLE THUMPED AS SHE TRIED TO open it.

"Not right now."

"Gloria." My mother's perfectly powdered face stared at me. Our eyes met through the shatterproof glass.

"I said, not right now. *God!*"

She backed off with a huff.

As Mom retreated into the house, I cracked the window. Just enough to let some fresh air invade the car, sweet smells of dogwood trees and azaleas. It was a scent I should have loved but couldn't. It reminded me too much of our home and all its memories. Loss hung over us like a thick curtain. And

219

as I watched my mother walk away, I cried.

After our talk on the bench in Georgetown, I couldn't stand to be around my mother. I felt like I'd stabbed her and then left the blade sticking out so everyone could see it. It hurt to think about. (As if that weren't enough, I'd totally abandoned Charlie. Right when we were starting to connect. I'd vanished. Dropped him like a bad habit.)

I suck.

A week had passed since I'd seen Charlie. In that time I'd managed to avoid everyone I knew. This included my family, whose busy lives usually kept them from bumping into me all that often anyway. In fact, I'd started to wonder if they'd even noticed I'd gone AWOL. Whole days passed with hardly a word. (They seemed fine with it; too fine, if you asked me.)

And it was when I figured I'd been forgotten that my mother began to stalk me.

She planned little ambushes. She executed sneak attacks along my daily route from the bedroom to the bathroom. It's a good thing I'm quick, and skilled in the cold shoulder. (That, of course, is a weapon I learned from her. Oh, the irony. It was thick enough to bottle.)

I reclined in the front seat of the Toyota. The nighttime DJ dedicated songs to all the lovers out there. I sipped coffee but didn't really want it. I just used it to keep my hands busy. The last thing I wanted was to write in my Freak Folio. In the last few days I hadn't touched it. The whole thing felt like a lie.

I'd written more about Charlie Wyatt than anyone I'd ever met. Each and every word had been wrong. More than that, they'd been unfair. He was different, sure, but he'd turned out to be the least freakish person I'd ever met. Why did I have to make everyone the enemy? It was the worst kind of cowardice.

My cell phone rang.

I glared at the screen. It was a number I didn't recognize.

All day I'd been holding out for one call. "Hope" might as well have been the name on the caller ID, as I watched the blue display blink. "Is it *him*?" I wondered silently to myself, with anticipation, with dread.

I answered.

"Gloria, this is your mother speaking," said the voice on the line.

I looked out the window. She was nowhere to be seen.

"What number is this?" I asked.

"It's my private work line," she said. "I knew you wouldn't answer the phone if I used the regular number. Now unlock the car and come inside."

"You were right, I wouldn't have answered," I said, and promptly hung up.

I knew she was hurting, but so was I.

She was living in a place where the past was the past. Everything tragic was safely behind her. Me, I was stuck in a world where my brother had just died. It was a place where every person, every stranger, offered potential heartbreak.

I wanted to be able to get close to someone again. More than anything else. But I was terrified. Before, I'd been afraid of knowing Charlie. Now, after running away, I was afraid I'd lost my one chance to do just that.

Curled in the driver's seat, I stared up through the sunroof. Stars pricked the sky in infinite clusters. I tried to visualize how small I really was. As if looking down from the heavens at Earth in reverse. I felt like a character in one of Maggie's comic books: a lost soul alone in her car, at a crossroads. That's always when the aliens visited. Or the radioactive disaster occurred. Or the magical amulet was discovered. Everything changed when the hero was at her lowest. When she was certain she'd reached the end.

I thought about superheroes, which made me think of Faris.

Why did I think he'd be mad at me for trying to get on with my life? He never would have wanted me to be so stuck. Not because of him. He would have taken one look at me curled up in the car and said, "The Academy Award is in the mail, Glory."

And when I heard my brother's sweet, lost voice in my head, the phone rang again. I looked down and saw the name I'd been waiting for, for seven days, six hours, and forty-two minutes.

EDISON, PAUL.

Charlie.

Then, and only then, did I unlock the door.

The next day, a Tuesday, I drove into DC, made a few stops. I wanted everything to be perfect. By the time I got to the National Mall it was around nine o'clock. Parking was a bitch, but when wasn't it? Damn tourists. I doubt this was what our Founding Fathers had in mind.

As if Abraham Lincoln hadn't been tall enough in real life, his nineteen-foot statue towered over me. I stood puny in his memorial, dressed in a tank top and black pigtails. The sunrise crept up the marble steps behind me. It painted the walls a rose-petal pink. It was morning and everything felt new again. No more running.

Raising my cell phone, I took a single picture of the light as it illuminated Lincoln's face. Not because he was inspiring. No. With all those wrinkles he bore a striking resemblance to my Aunt Cecilia. Maggie would need proof before believing me.

About halfway down the steps I got comfortable. I sat alongside the long metal railing. On my knees I balanced a picnic basket. The reflecting pool shimmered like foil. A group of ducks leaped from its surface. They soared across the Mall, quacks rising above the trees. I couldn't have asked for a more beautiful day.

"Gloria!"

I turned. A lean figure stood at the foot of the stairs. The walkway around him was spotted with bird poop. It was Charlie.

Springing up, I waved once. Then I clasped my hands in front of me, trying not to fidget. (Not to touch my hair, to make sure every strand was fixed in place.) "Hi," I called.

At first, he just kept waving. That's it. But I wasn't blind. I saw how his slouch straightened when our eyes met. How his frown curled up into a smile. How he changed.

Charlie climbed the monument toward me. In his hands he held a cardboard tray with two coffee cups. Despite all the tourists milling about, it felt very much like we were all alone—me, Charlie, and the Great Emancipator.

"Hey" was the first thing he said when he reached me. "I feel nauseous" was the second.

"Are you too sick for breakfast?" I asked. I pulled back the top of the picnic basket. There were muffins, fruit.

"Why?" he asked, setting down the coffees. "Not really hungry."

"Because," I said, "it's the most important meal of the day."

"And what a couple of days," he said, stuffing his hands into the pockets of his sweatshirt.

I'd never been happier to hear his voice.

"I needed to see you," he said.

"And I like being seen," I replied.

"I don't know why, really," he said. "I thought it might help."

Bending over, he picked up one of the steaming cups of coffee. He passed it to me. Our hands brushed against each other. (I hadn't been expecting him to get so close to me so quickly.) I nearly flinched as our fingers touched.

He sat heavily on the step next to me, grunting. Then he took a long drink. His eyes were bright red and bloodshot. The ends of his spiky hair drooped with day-old greasiness. And as we drank, Charlie didn't say a single word.

I'd never seen him like that. Charlie Wyatt, the boy who had a comment for everything, stared silently into space. He ignored the people taking pictures where Martin Luther King Jr. gave his "I Have a Dream" speech. He ignored the toddler in front of us who was taking off his pants and pulling down his diaper. Most surprisingly, however, was that he ignored me.

"I'm . . . I'm sorry, Charlie," I said. He must have been furious at me for walking out on him. I'd acted terribly. That was why I'd set up this rendezvous on the Mall. I wanted to show him that I wasn't a wimp, even if I often came across that way. I needed to know I was forgiven. That it was okay.

He turned to look at me with bloodshot eyes. "Sorry about what?"

Confused, I decided not to press him. "Don't worry about it."

"Talk to me about something," he said. "Tell me about your week, or tell me more about you. Talk to me about something good."

"Well, not much is going on," I said. "I have my mom's dinner in a week. I sure as hell don't want to go."

"I bet it'll be nice."

"I'm not in the mood to swank it up at some posh hotel on Sixteenth Street."

"What else?"

I shrugged. "Honestly, nothing good has happened."

"Then tell me about you," he said, closing his eyes. "*You're* good."

None of this was going as I'd imagined. He wasn't acting like himself, or as I'd come to know him. "Are you okay, Charlie?" I asked.

"Ask me a question," he said, dodging my query. "Ask me something you always wanted to ask someone."

I took the bait. "It can be anything, really?"

"Anything," he said, his gaze wandering.

I concentrated and tried to think of the deepest philosophical mystery I'd ever pondered. Instead, I thought about my nose. Yes, my nose. With all the cosmic conundrums spanning the universe, the first thing that came to mind was my looks. (I was surprisingly good at shallow.)

I put my coffee down and rubbed my hands together. Cars zipped over the bridge behind us. "You're good at honesty," I said, sliding my rings up and down my fingers. "So tell me, is my nose weird?"

Charlie took my hand, firmly but not forcibly, so that I stopped fidgeting. "Your nose?" he asked. He had a beauty mark in the corner of his mouth. I'd never really been that close to him before. Not in the brightness of day. "Your nose is perfect."

"You don't think it's too big?"

"No, I don't," he said, and then chuckled.

I took his hand. This time when we touched, it was like brushing exposed wires together—a spark. I lifted his hand to the spot on my nose where the cartilage made a small ridge. "This bump right here. You don't think it's . . . ugly?" It couldn't have been more than a centimeter of skin. You had to strain to see it. Still, it was enough. (I'd spent my childhood wishing for a cute button nose. Like the girls on TV had, a blob like a dollop of whipped cream.)

Charlie shrugged. "I always thought that bump was the best part. It makes you special—but in the beautiful way, not in a scary circus freak sort of way."

If anyone else had said this, it would have been different. But I knew him now. Every word came out exactly how he intended.

"You really think that?" I asked.

"Sure," he said.

His big spidery fingers enveloped mine. They hid the black nail polish. I turned one of his hands over in mine. It was rough, scratchy with calluses. And it shook.

"Charlie, tell me. What's wrong?" I asked.

It was still a pretty day. That hadn't changed. Pigeons pecked at potato chip crumbs at our feet. A group of Asian tourists passed by in matching yellow baseball caps. Far down Constitution Avenue, a police car blasted its siren. Then it roared off toward the white dome of the Capitol.

Our coffees sat at our feet, growing cold.

"I'm sick of feeling powerless," said Charlie. It was a sad sound, not like words but like one long sigh.

"Did something happen?" I asked. "You're acting weird."

He shook his head and took a huge swallow. "I always act weird," he said. "It shouldn't be some big surprise."

"You're acting *different*," I clarified.

"Nope, it's just me," he said, "regular old boring Charlie Wyatt, gazer of stars, maker of lunches, and master of customer-service bullshit." He chewed a muffin angrily, tearing it to pieces. "Whatever you think I am, I'm not."

"Well, I like you, whatever that is," I said. I wanted to touch his hand again, even as he pulled away.

"Do you?" he asked, turning on me. His voice had developed an edge, and it was a sharp one. "First you hated me, and

228

then you really liked me, and then you ran away." He snorted. "'Like me'—what does that even mean? You don't know anything about me."

"I'm starting to," I said, trying to calm him.

"I thought we were being honest," he said sarcastically.

Everything was going wrong. We sat right next to each other. It felt like miles. So I decided to make a move, to close that distance. Sliding an arm over his shoulders, I pulled him close. That's when I felt the lump.

A bundle of red fabric bunched up under his shirt. I pulled on the collar to straighten it for him. He didn't protest or even seem to notice. My pulling accidentally caused one of his front shirt buttons to pop open. As it did, I saw the bright triangular symbol underneath—Superman. He was wearing a cape.

It gave me chills. Not all of them good ones. I tried not to care.

"What've you got here?" I asked, gently squeezing his neck. I couldn't remember the last time I'd touched someone so tenderly . . . and not been related to them.

"Nothing," he said. "Sometimes you need a little extra help."

"What kind of help?"

He shook his head, frowning. "Listen. I'm not crazy," he said.

"I know," I said, "so tell me."

Turning to me, his face softened. His voice grew shaky. "When I was seven, I fell out of the tree in front of our house. That was back before we lived in an apartment. I sprained my ankle pretty bad and stayed home from school for a few days to keep off the foot—not that I was some kind of school athlete or anything, but, still, you know how kids are. I don't have many memories of what I did during all that time inside the house, but I do remember one thing."

He brightened, if only for the briefest of moments. "Mom took care of me, and one day she brought me a bag full of stuff from the store: an icepack, candy bars, and a copy of *Superman*."

I stroked his hand. "And you were hooked, right?"

"It was more than that," he said. "It was like I suddenly had a role model. My whole life I'd never really fit in, I felt like some kind of freak; I don't know why exactly, maybe because I talk a lot or because I get in people's personal space, or because I tend to think out loud instead of being careful, but for whatever reason, I've never really . . . *clicked* with other people.

"And then I read about Superman. Think about it. He's not even human, but he's also the greatest person on Earth. He's an alien . . . but has that ever stopped him from embracing humanity, from saving our sorry butts again and again? No.

If anything, his uniqueness drives him." He nodded, mostly to himself. "I realized that I could be different and still be me."

The white scar on his left temple flared brighter. Without permission, I lifted a single finger and touched it. I traced the line from his hairline to the bottom of his brow. He didn't speak or move. The way Charlie described him, Superman reminded me of my brother. Nothing discouraged him. He knew what he believed.

"It's a good message," I said.

"Ever since then I've been interested in astronomy," said Charlie, "in what lies out past where the human eye can see. Because whatever it is, there's a good chance it's worth looking for." He shrugged.

"I'll take your word for it," I said. Then I flashed him a smile.

He tried to return it. Really, he did. But something heavy hung over him. His expression contorted into something that wasn't a frown but wasn't a smile either. It was like his face had melted in the fierce morning sun.

"My mom," he said with some difficulty, "she's getting worse." That was it. He didn't say another word for several long minutes. It was as if he expected the words, now released into the wild, to float away, to pop like bubbles.

Then he added, "I knew it would happen, I just forgot." Tears welled up in his eyes. "Does that make me selfish? Is it bad to go on with your life, to make the best of what you've got?"

It was a question I'd been asking myself for a year. And I'd never had an answer.

"No," I heard myself say. And my voice sounded a lot like my mother's: strong, reassuring, even a bit wise.

He crumpled his empty cup in one hand. "I tried, Gloria," he went on. "I tried every day. I talked to her, to reach her in whatever dark place she went when she wasn't with us; but most of the time I know she probably never heard me." He took a deep breath. "Maybe I should just follow everybody's advice and keep my head in the clouds. You know? Leave old terra firma to the humans."

"No, you shouldn't," I said, leaning in. I had to keep pushing him, to get in close so he couldn't pull away. I knew how easy it was to retreat. And I wasn't going to let him. Not now. "You reached *me*, Charlie."

"What do you mean?"

"I haven't let myself be alone with anyone for a year," I explained. "If I get caught in a confined space with another person, I lose it. I panic. It's like they're radioactive. I don't want them near me."

"Why?"

I shook my fist at him. "I didn't want to get hurt." Then I laughed, amazed that we were even having this conversation.

"And I don't know if it's because you're an astronomer or what, but you showed me this big picture. Before, I never felt like I'd make it. The pain was always too huge. But you survived. You got to the other side of it. And if you could, well, then maybe I could, too."

We gazed at each other then as a huge posse of black-clad bikers clomped up the memorial steps around us, a parade of Hell's Angels on holiday. The veins stood out on the back of Charlie's hands. Like electric cords under a throw rug. His skin was sandpapery (and felt good against the smoothness of my palms). Our small spot on the steps felt totally isolated. We were all alone, but not.

"Gloria," he said, "I have something to tell you."

"What is it, Charlie?"

He scrunched his forehead and thought about his next words carefully. This should have been fair warning. (Careful was not part of his repertoire.)

"I entered an astronomy contest sponsored by the University of California Santa Cruz and was chosen out of a group of four thousand applicants to accompany researchers on an all-expenses-paid research internship at the unopened ALMA radio telescope array based in the Llano de Chajnantor Observatory in the Atacama Desert of northern Chile."

I stared blankly.

At first, I thought he'd misspoken. That perhaps the whole

wacky South American telescope fantasy was meant for someone else. When he didn't correct himself immediately, I realized he was on the level.

"That's fantastic," I said, breaking into an embarrassing chuckle. "Right?"

"I leave in two weeks," he blurted.

I blinked. It was like he'd flashed that giant spotlight of his directly in my eyes. "Wait . . . what?" I stammered. "Like, two weeks from *now*?"

"And I'll be gone for six months."

"What?" I said again, a broken record.

After everything he'd done: his relentless pursuit, his calls, his notes, his soul-baring rooftop exploits . . . following all that, he was going to run for the border? Didn't he understand? He'd gotten the girl. I was here; I was cute. Get used to it.

"Wow," he said. That one single word came out hollow. Like a sound effect. Based on the startled pall of his face, he was as disoriented as I was. He attempted to stand up. It was robotic. Wobbling, he needed to grasp the nearby railing for balance. "I need to leave," he whispered. "I think."

"How long have you known about this?" I asked after him.

But he didn't answer my question. He just stared down at me. Right away I knew what was happening. He had the look of someone trying to take it all in, to gather every minute detail and put it away for later. For a bad day when you wake up queasy or when you hate your job—or when you have to say good-bye to the one person you've found who matters.

"See you, Gloria," he said. "I have to go now."

"Charlie," I said, almost frantic.

His only reply was "Thanks for the muffins."

With that, Charlie Wyatt walked off.

As he did, I caught something in his weightless, drifting gait. Arms stiff, legs wide, he reminded me of an astronaut. He seemed to float. He seemed to wander, at the mercy of forces beyond his control. I'm sure he thought he was alone— miles from home.

But he wasn't.

FREAK

"HEY, CHARLIE, GIVE ME A HAND, MAN."

I sat on my stool behind the register, thinking, scanning my copy of *Foundations of Modern Cosmology* and sipping from an open liter of chocolate milk. The new logbook Gloria had given me lay open in front of me—tanned and leathery—with an even black crack down the binding. I was ready to work. New pen—check. Pretentiously fancy tassel bookmark—check. Personalized front-cover inscription that melted your heart every time you read it—check. All was in order, yet I'd been sitting that way for two hours and hadn't read a word of the text or jotted down a single note.

I once heard someone say that nothing was scarier than a

blank page. Of course, I couldn't remember who that "someone" was, meaning he could have been an ax murderer or a drunk or a dictator or just an all-around unpleasant person, so I probably shouldn't be listening to him in the first place. Besides, I could think of a lot of things scarier than an empty piece of paper—cancer, for one, and bears.

It wasn't hard to be dreary when every time you looked around, the world seemed to grow more depressing, the rain shining blacker, dark skies always threatening to blot out the blue, like a sponge cleaning up an accident. However, the longer I sat staring at the emptiness of the page, feeling useless, the more I understood what that saying was all about: Starting over was hard. That's why you needed to do it.

I thought about Gloria Aboud. Doing this made me feel light inside, as if someone were rubbing two sticks together inside my chest to make fire. That was nice.

Then I thought about how I was departing the country in less than two weeks, and I felt nothing. Every time I imagined actually stepping on that plane and dropping into that sweaty seat with the porthole window, I felt a little more confused, more distant from the world going on around me; it was like I was peering through the eyepiece of one of my telescopes, and no matter how I turned the focuser, nothing ever became clearer. In fact, the picture seemed to grow blurrier the more I thought about leaving.

Next to my perch on the stool, my coworker Arnold rang up customers as fast as his greasy little fingers could manage, which wasn't fast enough, since our two register lines—his and mine—had collided into a traffic jam of grumbling customers.

"Charlie!"

I ignored him.

People waiting to check out glared at me, but I didn't care. Let them smolder. As for Arnold, he could sweat in that hate for all I cared. Couldn't he see that I was busy? I needed to concentrate if I was going to get my groove back and wow the folks at ALMA with my discovery of an as of yet unconfirmed comet.

Arnold swiped a debit card and the scanner beeped, authorizing. "Give me a freaking hand, man," he hissed as the little machine chugged, awaiting a connection.

I continued to ignore him, instead choosing to contemplate Gloria, and signs, and how astrology and astronomy are quite similar, except that one is the objective gathering of information, while the other is an attempt to give purpose and prediction to that data. I'd never really considered the core similarities, at least not until Gloria. Really, how difficult would it be to take the leap from one to the other, from observer to dreamer?

"Charlie, please." Arnold struggled. The customers fumed. I did nothing.

Fridays were our toughest nights—between four and ten, without fail, our aisles teemed with people picking up their last-second supply of weekend toilet paper or an emergency bottle of children's Tylenol for Little Billy's peaking fever. Usually I liked seeing all the people out and about, but not that night.

Matching inflatable pool rafts in each hand, Arnold tried to enter in the item code with his elbow, but the scanner had quit reading and gone orange with an error sign. In his desperation and clumsiness, he ended up knocking a woman's purse to the floor and sending credit cards flying. "Charlie!" he said, turning to me, his face red and sweaty. "I'm asking nicely."

But I wasn't biting. What did any of this matter to me, anyway? Family Friends' problems weren't mine. They could all just go to hell.

Growing frantic, Arnold grabbed the bendable microphone sprouting from the counter and pressed a button. "Assistance required at the register, please," he said, voice shaky. "Assistance required at the register. Thank you."

Little Tommy appeared quicker than he normally did, and he scurried toward the counter in his windup-toy way, sliding the red vest over one arm as he came. He hardly made a sound, dressed in black leggings and ballet flats, a ninja. Now, I didn't know much about Little Tommy, but if he wasn't already in some kind of weird alternative rock band with a name like Fjord, he needed to join one as soon as possible, because it was his destiny. When he saw the register backup, his eyes grew huge.

"You're not ringing," he said. Was it a question or a statement? I wasn't sure. As always with the little guy, he was unreadable.

"Nah," I said.

"Can you take out your drawer, so I can put mine in?" he asked.

"Nah," I said.

Arnold easily pushed him aside and got up in my face. "I'm buried here, you ass," he said. "Help us."

"Charlie!"

Charlie.

I thought of how Mom used to call my name, before her voice changed to that of a total stranger's. Every time it was music. Now when she said my name I winced, because I knew it wasn't the person I loved saying it, but the dementia and the frog in her throat.

Charlie.

"Charlie!"

Arnold glared at me, but I kept staring at a spot on the counter that I'd chosen as my last stand, my Alamo. It was a blob of ketchup from my fast-food dinner, and it sort of looked like Greenland, if you squinted. Arnold cleared his throat dramatically, but I wouldn't break my gaze, never, not for him.

"Give me the code to your register drawer," he ordered.

"Nope," I said.

"Then give me the key."

"Sorry."

I couldn't change the things that really mattered, like what was happening to Mom, but I did have power over my stupid cash register. And I would not relinquish it. Not for Arnold. Not for anyone.

"Give it to me," he said, grabbing at the waist of my jeans. He must have assumed the key was in my pants pocket, when it was really stashed in the side of my shoe, wedged between my foot and the tongue. Hadn't he ever heard of pickpockets? "Give me the damn key, Charlie!"

At about this time, customers in line began to peel off and head for the front doors. I guess they'd waited long enough, and everyone knows there is a definite limit to how long you can stand in line listening to Kelly Clarkson and flipping through gossip magazines. This threshold clocks in at just shorter than the time you'd spend in a doctor's office waiting room, but a little longer than waiting for a table at a restaurant.

As they left, the people in line muttered about never coming back, and about the lousy service, things of that nature, but it didn't matter because plenty of new shoppers approached from the back of the store, oblivious to Arnold's public meltdown. That was the great thing about America. Someone always needed to buy toilet paper and Hi-C. People needed their crap.

"Now, Charlie!" He kept on molesting me, his slimy hands everywhere.

"Back off!"

"Give it to me, you weirdo."

I'd had it. I was about twice as big as Arnold, so I wrapped my arms all the way around his monkey body and hoisted him off me, setting him on the floor nearby.

Stepping back, he weighed his options, every muscle tense. He wanted to hit me but knew he couldn't, because he was deathly afraid of me, as he should have been. Instead, all he could do was squeak, "That's it," a sound that wasn't mad at all but almost childlike. "I'm getting my dad." Then he shuffled backward out through the saloon doors at the side of the counter and marched down Aisle Two toward the stockroom, an untied shoelace dragging behind him.

I got no joy from this victory. In fact, it just made me feel worse.

I felt a tap on my shoulder, and I turned and almost got lost in the enormous Disney cartoon eyes of Little Tommy. "Everything okay?" he said in a monotone voice.

Little Tommy may have or may not have been baked out of his gourd, I wasn't sure, but either way, he made those people in line wait even longer with their toaster strudels and bedpans and didn't lift a finger for anyone until he made sure I was okay.

If I hadn't felt so hollow, I would have hugged him. "I'm okay," I said.

"Do you want anything?"

I wanted so many things.

I wanted to scream my head off.

I wanted to punch Arnold in the face.

I wanted to touch my mother and make her whole again.

I wanted to run away to South America.

I wanted to hold Gloria's hand forever.

I wanted to be a stronger person than I was, than I had any right to be.

They say one person can change the world, but that's only true if you're powerful, if you can fly or lift trains from their tracks or run faster than the speed of light. Last time I checked, I couldn't do any of those things. I could barely even hold on to my pathetic job or get a girl to like me without freaking out and sabotaging the whole thing by wearing a superhero costume that was a size too small. There I was spending my beautiful summer day behind a dirty counter, wearing a red vest and a button that said MY NAME IS: CHARLIE. CAN I BE YOUR FRIEND TODAY? I was a joke.

"Nah, I'll be okay," I told Little Tommy, lying.

That's when Mr. Pastore arrived. I turned to find him standing right beside me, as though he'd teleported in with a puff of smoke and the smell of brimstone. The glare off his balding head was incredible, so clear you could read the names of the products reflected in it: Energizer batteries, Supercharge herbal enhancer, Orbit gum. He was a walking billboard.

"What's going on out here, Charlie?" he asked forcefully. Clearly the stress was getting to him, the grumpy customers with one foot out the door. "Why didn't you listen to Arnold?"

"Because he treats me like dirt," I said, "and he always has."

This caused Mr. Pastore to narrow his eyes at his son, who lingered by the photo department pretending to alphabetize the finished orders. But he turned back to me a second later. "Well, it's your job to come to his assistance," he said.

"Yeah, well, I don't like my job very much."

"Join the club," said Mr. Pastore, sighing and typing in his manager's override code and clearing the error from Arnold's register. The small orange screen returned to its default of 0.00. "You can't just stop whenever you want to."

"Sure I can," I said.

Waving to the next customer in line—a woman with a floppy white sun hat who was about as wide as a chest of drawers—he began to ring up her items without even making eye contact. He worked incredibly fast, a true professional. "That's not how the world works," he continued. "Problems will still be there, even if you turn your back."

"I want to go home," I said.

"Your shift doesn't end until seven."

"I'm not supposed to be here."

There was a rustling among the customers. "You should fire that kid!" someone—I didn't see who—shouted from the end of one of the lines. "He's lost it!"

"Just relax," Mr. Pastore called back to whomever, cracking a fake smile. "Things are moving along now. We apologize for the delay."

Then, showing the angry shoppers his back, he grew calm, as if everything going on had suddenly faded into the background, like one of those old movie matte paintings that made the actor seem a million miles away from the scenery. His voice remained steady as he spoke to me. "Charlie," he said, "your dad told me about the changes in your mom's condition." There was silence as he thought, and as more people fragmented from the mob and made their way toward the outside world. "And you've got to be strong, kid."

I didn't know anything about Mr. Pastore's personal life, but something in his voice told me that he understood where I was coming from. That he knew loss.

"I can't be that strong," I said. "I thought I'd found a way, but I was wrong."

"Then find a new way," he said.

And he turned to the next red face. "Now let's get back to work."

But what he didn't realize was that I would never sit in his squeaky office chair again. Not if I could help it. I didn't want to be some name-tag-toting, nine-to-five, Maui Sunset–dreaming stock blob. That was about the only choice I really did have: to wear or not to wear the red vest. And it was an easy choice. "If I don't, are you going to fire me?" I asked him.

Good old Mr. Pastore winked at me and then gazed out at the last few impatient frowns, his shoulders slumped into their usual default position, meaning closer to his waist than to his head. "Not a chance," he said at last, and then gave a little shrug that was oddly reminiscent of one of my own.

"Then I quit," I said.

And that's how I ended my three-month career at Family Friends neighborhood pharmacy, where the prices are low, and the smiles are free. I threw my own ass out the front doors, leaving a mob of disgruntled employees and patrons behind me.

And that's what it means to "go all Charlie."

* * *

Mr. Pastore had been right. I'd never be strong enough. All along, these last eight months, I'd been more Clark Kent than Superman, and I'd been hiding behind a big red *S*. Like my ex-boss said, my only option was to find a new way—a way out.

I sprinted home, not stopping for lights or pedestrians or to catch my breath, and at one point I tripped on a sprinkler that some genius had snaked across the sidewalk—a *public* sidewalk—and nearly got a compound fracture, the kind where your bone sticks right out of your skin like a busted twig, but luckily I fell up against this parked BMW with a flat tire and only bruised my shoulder, although I did set off the car alarm. I ran and ran, and by the time I reached the driveway of the apartment building, I was just getting warmed up but had no place left to run.

I shot past the security desk, and the guard listening to his iPod, and turned down the hallway leading to the stairs. The heavy door slammed behind me as I jumped the whole group of steps leading to the first landing, my arms out like huge hooks on the railings, yanking me up, higher. Rounding the corner, I shot up the next set of steps, three or four at a time, and raced past floors five and six and seven, not slowing down but starting to feel the burn. My hands were getting slippery. The stairwell was stuffy and hot, and as I bounded up the stairs between floors eight and nine, I tripped, knocking my right knee against the knobby twist in the railing. Down I went.

But I got back up right away. The sharp pain in my knee was like a whirling dentist's drill, but it was nothing, really. I was bigger than that, than pain. Agony was all a matter of perspective, or so I'd heard in some ad for a sports drink.

When my leg finally gave out on me, I was cresting the tenth floor. I didn't have any say in the matter at all, which surprised me, a lot actually, and I fell, again, sideways, my head dinging against the second-to-last step causing stars.

And this time I stayed down.

Slowly, I dragged myself the last few feet to the flat concrete landing and then into the corner of the stairwell. Stuck between floors nine and ten, I pressed my face up against the cool white blocks of the wall and felt the whole building hum with life.

I didn't want to stop, but I didn't know what to do anymore. Somehow when I wasn't paying attention, everything just got sort of too big for me to even dream of dealing with. I couldn't leap a tall building in a single bound. I couldn't even reach the mezzanine level without dry heaving.

I waited there in the corner, crying until someone a few floors up opened the stairwell and started coming down, forcing me to man up and wipe my eyes with my now useless red vest—a waste of twenty bucks, to be sure.

I got up and hobbled the remaining few stairs to the tenth-floor entrance. Every time I put weight on my right leg, it howled. A purplish bruise had begun to form on the ridges of my kneecap, and it changed shades when I poked it. I managed to reach the end of the hallway and our door, and slipped inside number 1056 unnoticed, or so I thought.

I walked down the hallway to my room, entered, and locked it.

A second later I heard Dad's heavy footsteps thump across the thin floor of the apartment, stopping in the hall outside.

"Charlie, that was Lou Pastore on the phone," said Dad through the door.

"And what did he want?" I asked, pulling my big canvas duffel bag out of the closet. "He's already taken my soul. All I've got left are fallen arches and astigmatism."

Dad knocked, softly at first, but then louder. "He told me what happened."

"Oh yeah, what did he say? That I'm crazy?"

"He's worried about you, Charlie."

I laughed. "I am no longer in his employ."

"Talk to me, Charlie!" said Dad, raising his voice.

"No!" I yelled. "I'm taking a vow of silence!"

I was done talking. I was a man of action.

Yanking open my drawers one by one, I emptied their contents messily into the top of the bag, not bothering to pick up the clothes that missed the opening and fell wrinkled to

249

the already cluttered floor. There was no time to stop and color coordinate, or to consider the hottest fall fashions in the indigenous Atacama Desert; no, this was survival of the wardrobe fittest—if an outfit managed to end up in the duffel, it was going to embark on a seven-hour voyage to the Llano de Chajnantor Observatory.

"Charlie, let me in!"

The last key component was underwear, but there wasn't an inch of room left in the duffel, so I had to settle for the pair of boxers I was currently wearing. I'd already worn them twice that week—turning them inside out for day number two—but they were a good pair and would see me through the cold nights. Or they'd just disintegrate after a month in a climate so dry it gets one millimeter of rainfall a year.

I cinched the top of the bag and headed for the door but hesitated when I passed my Maksutov. The telescope's long black tube pointed at the window like a dog hoping to be let outside. I knew I couldn't leave it there.

When I finally threw the bedroom door open, I nearly took off my dad's head, as he'd been leaning in close to listen to the movements inside.

I walked right by him, down the hall, out the front door, and in the direction of the elevator. I didn't stop, not even when he followed me to the dead end, where the fire hose sat behind its glass on one wall and an open window looked out over the Potomac on another. I pressed the down button and waited. The car dinged as it came—one floor, the next, working its way up.

"Where are you going?" Dad asked.

"I'm leaving," I said.

"Charlie, just relax," he said, and took a step, arm extended.

"I don't do 'relaxed.' You should know that."

"Then be reasonable."

"Again, we're talking about *me* here."

This time he got stern and stepped closer. "Put the damn bag down now!"

I leaped back, pulling out the Maksutov. For some reason—and I don't know why—I held it out the window; and I actually considered dropping it, and got excited at the idea of all that glass and metal scattering, getting caught in lawn mower blades for years afterward. "Stop or the telescope gets it!" I shouted.

"I don't understand," said Dad, stepping back, confused. "Stay away from the window."

That's when I caught the glint in his eyes—of complete and overwhelming fear. "I'm not going to jump," I said, and I laughed. "I'm not insane!"

"That's all fine and good," said Dad, not entirely convinced.

"Do you really think I'd jump ten stories? I'm not psychotic."

It was his turn to laugh. "I know you're not going to jump. But why would you want to throw your telescope out the window?"

I wrestled with this. I bit my lip and thought. "I don't want it anymore."

Again, he laughed. Everything was suddenly hilarious to dear old dad. "Charlie, you mowed three hundred lawns to raise enough money to buy that telescope. You cried when you finished putting it together."

I shrugged and wiped my eyes. "Good point," I said, sniffling. Damn logic, it gets me every time.

He got a few feet closer to me and nodded down at the duffel bag sitting lumpy and crooked at my feet. "Getting packed a little early, aren't we?" he asked.

"I figured I'd leave tonight," I said.

"Tonight?" he asked incredulously. "Why?"

"The sooner, the better," I said.

The elevator dinged to my left, and we both turned to watch the doors open. Neither of us stepped into the car, but Dad did reach over with one hairy arm and tap the *L* button for the ground floor. Groaning, the doors—and my window of opportunity—closed with a quiet thump.

Dad pushed his Redskins cap back on his head. "You're

worried about how things are changing," he said. It wasn't a question. "You were never good with transitions."

This sounded like an insult, and it angered me. Did he really know me as well as he thought he did? Could he have predicted that I was going to come home, pack my bags, saunter down to the elevator, and then threaten to toss a two-thousand-dollar piece of equipment down into Lee Highway traffic? He didn't have a clue.

"Do you want to know why I bought this telescope, Dad?"

He shifted his weight. "I know why. You love Superman. You love the sky."

"Wrong," I said, hating the feeling of the cold cylinder in my grip. Again, I wanted to watch it glide down to the black expanse and explode out of sight below. "I wanted it because I had to find a way out of this place."

"What do you mean by 'this place'?"

"What do you think I mean?" I shouted. "I couldn't leave the apartment because the only person who seemed to understand me was Edison, but there was no way I was going to survive spending all my time up here with all this . . ."

Dad relaxed back on his feet, not seeming panicked anymore, just sad. "All this what?" he asked.

"I had to go someplace else sometimes, Dad, to escape. And I just happened to find it up there." And I gestured to the open window with its cheap curtain waving gently across the windowsill like the hem of a certain pretty white dress worn by a particular girl whose name will not be mentioned.

"I understand," said Dad. "I know that feeling. We're not as different as you think, even if it feels that way sometimes."

"I couldn't stand it," I said. I didn't know what I was even saying anymore.

"What couldn't you stand, Charlie?" he asked. "The sadness, the hardship, the—"

"The *reality*," I said suddenly.

As I admitted this, I knew what I meant. On the mornings when I felt the need to don my Superman costume the most, when the red buzz of the baby monitor felt like it was coming from inside my head, I didn't want to accept the single irrefutable truth that this was the life I had, and that it wasn't going to suddenly cease belonging to me. It was a terrifying dead end to see waiting for you at the end of every day.

I set the Maksutov back down on the hallway carpet, mount and all, and then leaned against the wall, exhaling a breath that felt as if it would never stop coming out. "I was seven when we got the diagnosis, Dad. *Seven*."

Reaching up, he slid his ball cap back and forth on his remaining patch of hair, which highly resembled some of the more craterous areas of the moon's surface. "Like I could forget," he said. "I was there, too, remember?"

"Of course I remember."

Dad walked to the telescope, brown overalls streaked with white paint from where a contractor was adding a second coat to the lobby railings. The tiny black wireless headset still clung to his ear despite the fact that he'd officially clocked out three hours ago; of course, we both knew that Dad never went home from work, because his home was his work, and more often than not the two blurred, inseparable.

It occurred to me then that I'd never once seen my dad go to pieces over what had happened to my mother. There had never been a midnight confession over the kitchen table, no early-morning crisis at the wheel of the car, as he sobbed through his hot cup of joe. None of that BS you catch in the movies. If he ever fell apart at all, he did it in private and saved only the strongest stuff for me. All I ever saw was a brave face.

He fiddled with the telescope, turning the focuser. "You've got to keep in mind that how you see things depends on who you are," he said softly. "Take this telescope. When *you* look through this lens, you see celestial bodies and white dwarfs and black holes and whatever else you write down in your little book. Me, I see spots of white, a few spots of color, and a whole hell of a lot of black."

"I don't get it."

"When you think back to when we learned about your mother's disease, you probably remember a scared little kid looking for answers. Not me. I remember one tough little guy." He smiled at me. It was a man's smile, the kind he showed his old football buddies like Mr. Pastore or the big dudes who occasionally came to work in the boiler room. It made me feel older, and maybe even as strong as him.

"You do?" I asked.

"You're damn right I do," he said. "You did the best you could. The best anyone could have done. It was something to be proud of." He slipped off his hat and scratched his head. "And I was."

We stood across from each other in the hallway like two outlaws at the O.K. Corral, motionless, partners in crime who'd been through hell together but who still had a long way to ride. It was reassuring to know that we could overcome anything that came at us, because nothing could be worse than what we'd already been through.

All along I'd thought Dad didn't know me, but he did. I was the one without a clue.

"Come on," he said, hoisting up my bag. "Stay awhile."

I nodded and followed him back inside number 1056.

As we reentered, a voice called from the kitchen, "Where the fuck is everybody? You can't just leave a lady in here all alone, you pieces of shit!"

I closed the door behind me.

MAGNET

RAIN FELL ON THE CAR ROOF. DROPS TRICKLED DOWN THE WIND-
shield. I sat in park as traffic coasted through gathering
puddles. Everyone else was going somewhere. They passed
in wet swishes. Their tires threw up small waves of water. I
watched them go through the shimmer, jealous. Surrounded
by such a downpour, I couldn't help but cry.

Mom's big gala dinner started in two hours, and I looked
amazing—dressed to kill. I sat huddled with my back against
the door. I wore the white dress with the little yellow petals
on the hem.

Before me lay the only three letters Faris had sent me
from Afghanistan. I searched for comfort in the words, my

eyes so swollen I could barely read. The pages were worn thin from a thousand foldings and refoldings. All of them had been written on the same yellow legal pad. (A few even had the impressions from another letter still visible beneath the ink. Faint shadow letters twisted like rivers on a map.)

I had a memory of that notepad. It was from the night before his deployment. Sitting at the top of the stairs outside his doorway, I'd watched Faris pack. As everything else got shifted around—added, changed, replaced—that forgettable pad of yellow paper stayed on the top of the pile. For all I knew, he'd bought it at Family Friends. Maybe Charlie Wyatt sold it to him.

I'd lost Charlie, and I didn't know what that meant. Who was he? What if I'd had to describe him to someone? What would I have said? Charlie wasn't a stranger. Not much of an acquaintance, either. For me, Charlie had become something else entirely.

He was my friend.

We'd had almost two months of weirdness. And then, as abruptly as it had started, the affair was over. I'd phoned his house, left messages, but never a returned call. He was avoiding me because he had to leave. It was a tried-and-true method of not dealing with pain. And I knew how to do that almost better than anyone.

That's why I was crying. And why I was looking for advice

in letters that were two years old.

I was desperate. I hadn't eaten much in the last few days. Or taken a shower. Or left the house. Or changed out of the pink tracksuit with "Cat Fight" written across the fanny (a major Maggie-me-down).

With the volume turned low, I listened to a warped old mix tape Faris had made for me on my tenth birthday. All the songs were grossly outdated. Most of them were now background music in commercials. In between the songs, he'd recorded himself reading poetry. It was Naomi Shihab Nye, my favorite. The low growl of Faris's voice had always been that of a man's. Long before he learned to fix an engine or shoot a gun.

I wondered how long the recording would survive. Each time I listened, the quality suffered, the tape wore thinner. One day it would snap. Then it would be gone. Our one-way conversation would end for good.

I needed to talk to someone who could answer me. I needed to talk to Charlie.

It sounded like such a small thing, so easy. But it wasn't. Not for me. Reaching out meant everything. It's like that scene in bad movies, and equally bad commercials, when the naked guy sneaks out his front door to retrieve the newspaper and then gets locked out. There's a moment of commitment. Some call it the point of no return. You weigh your options and make a judgment call. Go naked, or give up. Me, I went naked. And now there was no going back.

Nature called. I slipped out into the misting rain and across the driveway. Then, in full stealth mode, I ducked into the house. In and out—that was how I'd do it. No one would even know I was there.

The entryway was dark, quiet. I lingered near the foot of the stairs. One hand rested on the smooth, polished banister. I'd never been a big fan of deserted houses. (Especially those you've held wakes in.) Every time it lay empty, that special eerie silence returned. Every time you were alone.

The upstairs floorboards creaked. The third level: Faris's room.

With that black cloud of despair hanging over me, I climbed the steps. No one was there. I walked the length of the hallway. Then I turned the corner and ascended the attic steps. For the first time in a year, I visited my dead brother's bedroom.

And that's where I found my mother.

She sat at the foot of the bed. Hands folded in her lap, she appeared to be praying; but I knew her better than that. She'd lost faith in God when an IED blew up her son's armored personnel carrier. As usual, she looked beautiful. She was dressed all in black, to celebrate this time. Not to mourn.

She hadn't noticed me, so I turned to go. Back to running.

Hell, I was good at it.

But she looked up when she heard the floorboards and looked right through me.

"Gloria?" she said, as if she wasn't sure it was really me.

"Hi," I said softly, stepping inside.

"Good afternoon," she said.

Nothing had changed in my brother's bedroom. You'd think this would have made it easier to be there. It wasn't. It was like bumping against a bruise you forgot about, only to get an aching reminder.

In junior high I thought Faris's room was the coolest. He'd hole up in there for hours at a time. When he emerged, it was always dressed hip, the center of a cloud of cologne. I just knew he was on his way someplace more exciting than where the rest of us might be headed. In that instant, with the door wide, I might catch a glimpse—of posters and the beaded curtains and the TV and shelves of comic books. Music trickled down the stairwell to where I stood gaping, like a member of his private fan club.

And I wanted it, all of it.

Now, though, the posters were curling. The CDs on the rack were bands that no one listened to anymore. (In fact, they were downright embarrassing.) The basketball player on the poster had long ago been caught in a drug scandal. It dawned on me then. That although Faris's room looked exactly as it had when he'd left, everything outside it had changed. So had I.

Mom watched me take in the surroundings. She waited for me to finish before speaking. "What do you see when you look at me?" she asked after an awkward silence.

I stared at my feet. They were shoved into a pair of Faris's old sneakers. (Even in a stunning dress I required comfort.) I didn't want to fight with her. Not in *his* room.

"I see my mom," I said.

"You say that like it's such a bad thing," she said, trying to smile. Her carefully assembled face trembled. As if the whole thing might come sliding off if she shed a tear.

"Maybe, sometimes," I said, trying to choose my next words wisely, "when it seems like you don't understand me." I crossed my arms. Faris's room was cool, and it felt hard to breathe. Maybe it was altitude sickness. We were on the third floor, after all. "You never even seem sad."

Her expression grew stony. "I know sorrow you cannot understand," she said.

Comments like those were what always got between my mother and me. It was like we were in a dark room with only a few candles. The wind kept snuffing out our lights, separating us in the shadows.

I thought about Charlie and his great big portable spotlight.

Walking up beside my mother, I touched her shoulder. "Tell me," I said. "I want to understand what it's like."

She took a deep breath. Her face stayed behind a curtain of glistening black hair. "I feel closer to him," she said. Her voice wavered. "He has been gone for more than a year now, Gloria. Yet his memory doesn't sadden me."

I wasn't sure what to make of this. "What do you mean?" I asked.

She looked up at me, smiling, which I didn't expect. "I mean that I remember him as he lived, as a happy boy. And that will always bring me joy, even in my worst moments. I will always have him near me."

"I'm glad," I said quietly. It was the nicest thing I'd said to my mother in months.

Then she parted her hair and I could see that she had actually been crying. Her makeup ran, oily black. "You are another matter, *habibi*," she said, using the Arabic word for "dear." Mom spoke Arabic only when she was deadly serious.

"How is that?" I asked.

"Your brother is gone, but he is here." As she said this, she touched her heart. "Imagine it. You live in a house with your daughters, but you feel farther from them than you do your dead son. Tell me, what does that say about a mother?"

As she talked, Mom absentmindedly picked through the

stuffed animals piled at the head of the bed. They hadn't been there when Faris lived in the room. Mom had put them there after his death. Plucking a sheep from the group, she held it.

"I have always been strong," she confessed, "but for *this* . . . I need to be more. Every day I face my failure."

I looked at her. My mother was the first woman in her family to attend college. She'd graduated second in her class from Harvard Law. Then she went on to be the first female partner in her law firm's history. In her personal time, she'd founded not one but three nonprofit institutions for the less fortunate. Even with all of that, she'd still managed to make us French toast every Thursday morning before school.

She was an incredible woman. She was a force of nature. She sat hunched on the bed like a little girl who'd just woken from a nightmare. And she was hosting a five-hundred-dollar-a-plate dinner in two hours.

"You could never be a failure," I said. "You're amazing."

"None of it matters if my youngest child hates me."

"I don't hate you. I just don't understand you."

A hint of her lightheartedness returned. "The feeling is mutual," she said.

We both smiled.

"You'll probably laugh at me," she went on, "but sometimes

I'm jealous of you."

I didn't laugh. Instead, I sat down gently next to her on the bed. "Why in the heck would you feel that way?"

"We feel the same things, but I don't have the words to express them. I wasn't born with them. Not like you were. Explaining how you feel is not the kind of thing a person learns in school or from her parents." Her smile became a smirk. "Especially not in your grandmother's family."

This made me laugh, even as my eyes filled with tears. My grandmother had been a ballbuster we called Sittoo. She didn't stand for weakness. Not one bit.

"You shouldn't be jealous, Mom," I said. "I'm a mess."

She wrapped an arm around me. Then she leaned a head on my shoulder. Like Maggie might do. "I would give anything to write one poem," she said.

I said the first thing that came to mind. "Maybe I can write one for you."

She kissed me on the top of my head. Our drippy noses practically touched. Her mascara ran down her cheeks, and she let it. "That would make me happy," she said.

Mom and Maggie waited for me in the car. They watched as I scurried across the busy parking lot. I was unable to break into a stride with my legs tightly wound in white fabric. Cosmetics clacked around inside my small black clutch.

Every time I hopped a puddle, my earrings jingled. It felt like everyone was looking at me even though there wasn't anyone around.

I entered the store and strode up to the counter. I smoothed down the front of my dress and pulled the hair out of my face. I'd applied a thin layer of makeup. The ingredients had been from both my mother's and sister's collections: eyeliner and mascara, courtesy of Mom; shimmery rouge and Whiz Poppin' Red lip balm, courtesy of Maggie.

The kid behind the register was the small elf boy I'd met before. He watched me get adjusted. When I was done, he said, "Whoa."

"You'd better believe this is worth a 'Whoa,'" I told him.

"Yeah," he said.

"Where's Charlie?" I asked.

Little Tommy stared at me blankly. "Charlie quit," he said. "Or maybe he got fired. I'm not exactly sure of the details, or at least I don't remember them."

"He doesn't work here anymore?"

"Yeah, something about his mom made him leave."

"Did he say what it was?"

"Only that she'd gotten worse," said Little Tommy. "I guess whatever it was just kind of knocked him out of his orbit." He shrugged. "It's a pity. I liked the guy."

"Thanks, Tommy," I said.

"No prob."

I folded my arms and stood underneath the giant "It's Grilling Time!" wiener that dangled above the entryway. I didn't know what to do next. It was getting late. The evening sun hung over the Arlington rooftops. It cast a warm orange glow across the sidewalks. My family waited for me in the car.

Life was not good, but it had the potential to be better. I wasn't afraid to reach out or to rediscover what was right in front of me. At least not as scared as I'd been. I knew that Charlie must be feeling a lot like I had, like suddenly, out of the blue, the Earth started spinning on a different axis. In one blink of an eye, everything you know changes.

It was Charlie who had taught me to start searching the darkness for a light—and if you couldn't find a glimmer, to be your own. I wanted him to know what that meant to me. That he'd taught me how to glow again.

That's when I had the idea. I was turning around to leave when I knew. A weird sense of calm came over me. I found myself wondering, What would Charlie do? In that frame of mind, nothing was out of the question. All things were possible.

"Can I go into your back room?" I asked Little Tommy.

"What?"

"Can you take me back there?"

His eyes widened. "This is just like a dirty dream I had," he said.

"Oh, stop," I said. "I want to get into Charlie's locker.

FREAK

THE SUN WAS ON ITS WAY DOWN, AND AS I SAT THERE SIPPING JUICE and aligning the finder on my old Tasco telescope, I watched it hang above a tall building like a halo. Daylight faded along with its peaceful peach color, and despite the coming darkness and the inevitable loneliness and the fact that I'd spent all the money from my last paycheck on expensive, but necessary, motion-sickness medication for the coming flight (at least Little Tommy was nice enough to give me my employee discount), I tried to look on the bright side. At last the rain had stopped, for a while, anyway. It was turning into the first clear night in weeks.

My little rainbow tent had mostly collapsed. It now hung

saggy and deflated on its four scrawny plastic legs like a punctured beach ball. I'd pulled the lawn chairs out from under the wet and drooping roof and sat in one of them with the open Styrofoam cooler between my feet. The rooftop smelled like mold. I'm pretty sure this was a result of the damp tent, which had been left out in the rain for almost a week straight, and which was never meant for strenuous outdoor activities but rather for children's birthday parties and sleepovers. Of course, as far as I was concerned, a tent was a tent, and any claim to be anything else was false advertising.

Sure, it had only cost thirty dollars and ninety-nine cents and I should have known better. Nothing for thirty dollars and ninety-nine cents lasts. It's not meant to.

I'd been hanging out on top of Family Friends a lot over the last few days, even after quitting my job there. Mr. Pastore didn't seem to mind. I actually think he enjoyed having me around, just not as an employee. I did less damage that way. There was something I liked about sitting high on that graveled rooftop. Sure, our apartment was lodged in a corner of the building's tenth floor, but there's nothing like having a view without any windows between me and the rest of the world.

From my perch, I was able to see each and every car that pulled in or out of the strip mall parking lot, and as I sat there sipping, I noticed one car pull out onto the street, its interior packed full of women. A stray arm dangled from an open window, a whirl of dress and hair and a glint of jewelry. It made me think of Gloria and our evening in the rain when all the stars seemed to align and we'd kissed.

So much for signs.

Sometimes that night seemed like a dream, like it had never occurred, not because it hadn't but because something that exciting wasn't the kind of thing that really happened, especially to a guy like me. Slouching in my saggy lawn chair, I wished it to be night. At least then I'd have something to look at.

With a rusty groan, the trapdoor to the roof opened suddenly and a small head appeared like a prairie dog's popping through a hole in the sand. It was Edison, the boy with bum legs, yet there he was on a roof twenty feet above the ground, like magic.

"Hey," he said, pulling himself over the edge of the ladder onto the gravel.

I didn't react. I didn't feel like talking. I'd recently decided to do less of it. I found that the more often I opened my mouth, the more often I got into trouble.

"I hope it's okay that I'm up here," he said. "The manager downstairs told me where to find you. I have to admit, it's pretty cool that he still lets you come up here even after you

271

quit. What is it, like severance or something?"

Scooting along the gravel, Edison traveled the few feet between tent and trapdoor and then came to a rest against the silver duct next to me. He exhaled and lifted the front of his shirt so he could mop the sweat from his forehead, and then he propped his legs up so his knees were bent and he looked normal. He always did this when he wasn't in his chair, which was pretty seldom. After getting situated, he waited a moment, elbows on those wobbly kneecaps, and then asked, "You okay?"

I didn't answer.

"Hey, man, you could at least acknowledge my existence," he said. "Nobody else knew where to look. Your dad didn't think you'd show your face here again. It just goes to show who spends more time with you." Laughing, he reached over and took the half-empty juice box from where it sat near my feet, and he took a long drink, still a bit out of breath.

He went on. "Oh, and in case you hadn't noticed, I usually travel on wheels, yet here I am on top of a roof accessible only by a ladder." He pretended to scratch his chin in deep contemplation. "Interesting. That would mean I would have had to drag my full body weight up three stories. I'd call *that* a testament to friendship."

He had a point. "Did you really climb up here?" I asked quietly.

"No," he said. "I took the elevator."

"They have an elevator?" I asked, shocked by the revelation.

Edison reached over and punched me in the shoulder. "Charlie, there's no elevator," he said. "Nada lift."

I shrugged. "I guess you're right. For a handicapped dude, you've got a pretty serious upper body."

"Got to," he said. "Without legs, the rest of me has to pick up the slack."

"I wonder if they'll have a weight room at the observatory," I said, realizing that I knew very little about where I was going.

Edison shrugged. "Maybe you can bench-press boulders or something. Impress all the egghead chicks."

"Maybe." I wondered. To me—and most guys I knew, meaning Edison—girls were as mysterious and complicated as some lost artifact that's just recently been uncovered, and no scientist in the world has ever seen anything like it and therefore doesn't even know where to begin decoding its signals. There was no Rosetta stone for chicks.

With Gloria, I didn't need to overthink. I missed her, her face and her voice, the way she said my name.

"What are you doing here, anyway?" I asked.

"I wanted to come and admit my failure," he said. "Isn't that big of me?" He started to pull himself up into the lawn chair next to me, and I reached over to steady it for him since they were flimsy, a fact I'd proved time and time again.

As he got comfortable, the sweat starting to soak through the front of his shirt, Edison smacked me in the shoulder. "I believe I may have led you astray, old boy," he said.

"Why do you say that?"

"Because I rained on your parade," he said, laughing as if at some private joke I wasn't in on. "I've known you for what, eight years, and you've never once talked to me about a girl. Then, one day, you do." He tapped his chin. "And what does the best friend suggest? Why, he convinces you to forget about it and focus on an unpaid internship in a country where the spiders are as big as your hand. It's genius!"

I laughed, but shook my head as I did. "No. You were right. The ALMA trip is a huge honor. It'll do wonders for my career if I end up going into astronomy as a profession."

But then it was he who was shaking his head. "Screw it," he said.

"No, really," I went on. "There's a natural order to things. Gloria and I don't work because we don't make sense. Destiny has no basis in science."

Edison nodded as he listened. "You know," he said, "you're not the only one who reads books, smarty-pants. After our little talk a few weeks ago, I did some research of my own."

"Oh yeah?"

"It's called 'spontaneous order.'"

"Never heard of it."

"It's a real theory. Been around for thousands of years, they say."

"So what?"

He smiled and waved his arms, implying everything and nothing in particular. "It states that some of humanity's greatest developments were created out of total chaos. The best kind of order cannot be planned, or created. It only comes about by adapting little by little to factors out of your control."

"That's heavy," I said.

"That's *life*," said Edison. "One thing I've learned from dealing with these"—and as he said it, he gestured to his legs, which lay beneath him looking absolutely normal but were in fact totally worthless—"is that the only way to have a future is to first see yourself having one."

Put that way, it sort of made sense. "So your world is what you make it, literally."

"Impose your own order, man," said Edison with a shrug.

I looked up at the afternoon sky, with its darkening edges and emerging moon. "Well, maybe that's good for other people, normal people, but not me."

Edison bent his finger to summon me closer. "Charlie, I have a secret for you," he said as he suddenly wrapped an arm around my neck and hugged me tightly. "You're more normal than you think."

I'd never had a brother, but having Paul Edison as a friend gave me a pretty good idea of what life might have been like if I had.

"Come on," he said. "Let's go downstairs and get something to eat. I hear the new Chinese place two doors down won't make you puke. That's a major improvement over the last place we tried."

"Maybe tomorrow," I said, standing up.

"More food for me," he said with a shrug.

With one foot propped on the cooler and my hands on my hips, I stared out over Arlington, Virginia, my home, and wondered what—if anything—would be different the next time I saw it. Six months was a long time to be away, especially with how fast the world seemed to change.

Edison whistled, and I turned to see him watching me. "Sometimes you do look a little like Superman," he said.

Not saying a word, I grabbed the collar of my shirt with both hands and tugged gently. The top button slipped free, revealing nothing but 100-percent grade-A Charlie Wyatt underneath.

At that very moment my replica Superman costume and cape were up for sale on Hot Hollywood Re-creations, the auction site where I'd originally purchased them. I was hoping to recoup that four hundred and fifty dollars; although I would have taken less to account for wear and tear.

Being a superhero was a dirty job, but somebody had to do it.

I walked out the sliding glass doors of Family Friends and into an evening of soft blue and purple, and it was as if I were the first man to step onto the remote surface of Mars—that is, if the red planet had a giant recycling bin sitting off to one side, a line of cars parked out front, and a group of chain-smoking teenage occultists who hung around behind the new Chinese takeout place listening to speed metal on someone's laptop. Other than those things, it would have been just the same, like, exactly.

A few steps after we exited the automatic doors, Edison took his leave, but before he did, he patted my butt and circled me in his chair. "Keep your chin up," he said, "and I'll see you this Sunday, suitcase in hand."

"Actually, it's more of a giant duffel bag," I corrected him.

"I don't care what it is," he said, "it's getting chauffeured by me."

Then he rolled down the ramp onto the recently repaved asphalt, in and around college girls walking to their cars in flip-flops, hands full of kung pao and lo mein. Not once, but twice, he paused to examine a girl from his unique, low vantage point, before continuing across the parking lot.

As I watched him go, I heard a quiet cough of someone

trying to get my attention, and I turned around.

Behind me, wearing a puffy vest over a long-sleeved T-shirt and an old 1940s newspaper delivery-boy hat, stood Little Tommy, hands jammed in his pockets, eyes peering out from under a curtain of dyed black bangs.

"Hey," said Little Tommy.

"Hey, man," I said. "You should catch Edison. He's going over to Mandarin Mania to grab dinner. I hear their stuff won't mess you up." I'd always liked Little Tommy. Maybe he could keep Edison company when I was gone.

"Nah, nah," he said, brushing his bangs out of his eyes. "I just wanted to give you this before I crushed it or ate it or something."

This wasn't the most appealing preface, but I understood better what he meant when he handed me something out of his pocket. It was a folded origami box made from a piece of paper. I instantly recognized the handwriting on the page as Gloria's. The visible words on the sides of the cube, scrawled in that familiar script, read: *I wonder where the talk would have gone between him and me.* When I took the cube, something rattled inside it.

"What is it?" I asked.

"It's from that girl," he said, "the pretty one."

Heart beating fast, I opened it, peeling back each pointy layer. There, sitting in the tiny cup of my palm like a nugget of gold in a muddy stream, was a small purple heart. She'd taken it from my bag of discounted, thrown-out merchandise, the one I'd told her about that day in Aisle Five.

And I did.

ARIES
3/21–4/19

Skies are clear. It's time for a change.

FREAK MAGNET

I TOOK THE SUBWAY, *AND* TWO CABS, AFTER PAYING SOME GUY IN the Metro station ten dollars for a map of a completely different part of town than where I was going simply because I couldn't get him to leave me alone, and none of these things I'd ever done before in my life, and none were things I would have done if I hadn't been trying to reach Gloria.

The reason I'd needed two cabs was because the driver of the first, a Kenyan man named James, wearing small round glasses and a Yankees cap, had gotten so sick of my company that he'd screeched over to the curb in front of the National Archives and asked me to get out of the car, remarking that it was the first time in his seventeen-year career that he'd ever refused a fare.

He told me, quite candidly, that I talked too much.

What can I say? I was excited.

The hotel was huge and regal and like something out of an espionage thriller where an assassin holes up on a rooftop and tries to shoot a man carrying a trove of national secrets in a microchip so small he can lodge it between his teeth and gums, or in another tight spot I'd care not to mention. It was certainly a place I never could have afforded, assassinated or otherwise.

I got out of the second cab on Sixteenth Street and jogged across the crosswalk to get to the opposite side, where a line of limousines jammed the semicircular driveway leading to the front entrance of the hotel and where valets bustled along the sidewalks waving key chains in the air and shouting to one another in Arabic. Men in tuxedos and women in beautiful gowns walked the plush red carpet into the revolving door, lit by the hazy glow of a chandelier.

Slipping by mostly unnoticed, I got into the lobby without much trouble, and I can only assume it was because I was the only person there wearing pants that cost less than two hundred and fifty dollars. Past the doors, a grand marble staircase led up to the next level, and at the foot of the steps stood a sign that said "Gala Upstairs."

Adjusting my clip-on tie, I began the ascent.

At the top of the staircase I encountered a small table lined with red velvet ropes and stanchions, and behind it waited a young guy with a goatee and a constipated expression on his face. He held a clipboard with a pen and a small stack of slightly ragged pages on it, and in his ear he wore one of those special headset receivers that was so small you wondered if he even knew it was there, as if someone had stuck it on him as a practical joke and he hadn't caught on yet.

The guy looked me up and down. "Excuse me, sir. May I see your ticket, please?"

"I have to get in there," I told him.

"Ticket, please," he repeated.

"I don't have one," I said, "but I have to get in there."

"No, you don't, kid," he said. "If you had to get in there, you'd have a ticket."

"I wore this suit," I said, stepping to one side like a fashion model, so he could see how good I looked in Dad's old corduroy sports coat and black dress shoes. I'd even gone so far as to buy cuff links from Family Friends for four dollars and ninety-nine cents.

The guy at the table surveyed the "Charlie Wyatt Look" one more time and then said, "I'm sorry, but even if you had a ticket, this event is black-tie."

"I can get a black tie, no prob." Then I thought about it. "Or I can just get a black marker and color this one. I don't care about it that much. I found it in a public bathroom."

"I'm sorry," said the guy.

"Come on, man," I said. "I want to see a girl in there. You know what that's like, right?" I wanted to tell him that despite the fact that he appeared to be completely unlovable, he still must have known what it felt like to have to see that one special person more than anything, and how nothing could get in your way, not mountains or barbed wire or visa restrictions or a really persistent doorman like him, but then I started to wonder if the guy even had a significant other in his life, since he looked pretty hollow-eyed and stressed and maybe even infected with something.

All of this came to mind to speak, but I didn't speak it. Instead, I looked him in the eyes and said, "Let me through. *Please.*"

Sternly he shook his head, and I swear that for a second he seemed to be enjoying himself. "Nah," he said.

"Someone get Gloria!" I said loudly to the passersby.

"Keep your voice down, sir," hissed the guy, glancing around.

"Gloria!" I shouted again at the top of my lungs. After trying to do it the right way, I was now going to do it *my* way.

"Sir, I'm going to call security," said the guy.

"GLORIA ABOUD, WHERE ARE YOU?"

"Sir!"

"GLORIA!"

Since my arrival, one senator, two TV actors, and three foreign potentates had taken the small stage. All of them had said generally the same thing. Together they had wasted ninety minutes. (Call me crazy, but I didn't need a former star of *Friends* crying to me about a refugee crisis.) So I'd left the banquet hall.

The volunteer booth suited me better. I sat next to a few college students, the three of us in fancy dresses. I took names for the mailing list. Wrote handwritten thank-you notes to recent contributors. We cracked jokes about all the cleavage on display.

I'd spent years helping Mom. And she always insisted on actual signatures. No mailer ever hit the post office without a human being's name scrawled on it. Faris, Maggie, and I had done this since the beginning. Back when the foundation was a gig run out of our family room. We called them "ghost autographs" then. Mom insisted on the little things. (Personal touches went a long way. A tip she'd learned from her own mother.)

After a particularly busy fifteen minutes, the doors to the banquet hall opened. People left their tables to use the restrooms or fetch cocktails. The waiters and bartenders scrambled back into position. A new wave of volunteers arrived to relieve me and my comrades.

Maggie stuck out from the crowd in her green satin miniskirt and knee-high go-go boots. She got a lot of odd looks as she crossed the hall toward me. Mostly from people who didn't work with our mother. Those who hadn't known Maggie since she was five years old and watched her eccentricity mature into monstrosity.

At her arm was a gangly guy with a thin beard who was dressed in a powder blue seersucker suit. It was clearly thrift-store variety. And he was clearly Pill, the comic-book guru and on-again, off-again boyfriend. Consider me amused. Unimpressed but amused.

Pecking him on the cheek, Maggie sent him for drinks. Off he loped, a hippie gazelle. Then my sister sashayed up beside me.

"*That's* what all the fuss is about?" I asked, leering at her date.

"Shoo," she said. "He makes me laugh."

"Me too," I said. "I can't stop."

She ignored me. "I'm hungry," she said, inserting an entire mini quiche into her mouth.

"You haven't stopped eating since we got here," I reminded her. "You might want to keep it in check if you're heading back to school in the fall. You don't want to return to campus with the 'Senior Seventeen.'"

She slugged a drink of white wine. "Doesn't matter," she

said. "Besides, I'm obviously going more for the 'Senior Seventy.'"

"Hey, will you watch my stuff?" I asked her as I stood up. Felt-tip markers had blackened my fingers. I didn't want to muss anyone's fancy manicure with a handshake.

"Sure," she said. As I walked away, she suddenly grabbed my arm. "Name tag!" she declared. "Unless you're going to a mixer in the john, I'd suggest losing the sticker."

"Yeah, thanks," I said, and stripped the sticker from my dress. It left a rectangle of residue that I picked at as I made my way to the bathroom. I glanced up every few steps so I wouldn't collide with a member of Congress.

Locking myself in a stall, I found my first peace of the night. There was only enough room for one person in there.

It was a weird place to think about Charlie. But I did. I wondered if he'd gotten my message.

That's when I heard someone shouting my name. I could hear it clear as a bell all the way in the bathroom, third stall down.

It's bizarre hearing your name yelled across a crowded hotel lobby. Not very different from hearing someone calling after you in a busy public garden, I guess.

Jumping to my feet, I yanked down my dress. Then I sprinted out of the bathroom without even glancing in the mirror.

I was still fixing my underwear when I neared the steps and saw them. Saw *him*.

Charlie stood next to a security guard at one of the gala entrances. He wore a rumpled corduroy suit and a pair of black pants with an elastic waistband. On his feet he had two loafers. Around his neck dangled a tie with a picture of a sunset on it. For all his many wrinkles, I'd never seen someone cuter.

I approached. As I did, I tossed my hair back and tried to look fabulous. This was my family's party. I was an ambassador.

"What's going on here?" I asked the anal-retentive guy working the ticket table. When the guy wasn't looking, I shot Charlie a smile. He grinned back at me before turning away sheepishly.

"He was trying to get in without a ticket," the guy explained. "I was telling him that he can't loiter, as there are dignitaries present and security is very high."

"Let him in," I demanded. "I'm Gloria Aboud. My mom runs the foundation."

"If that's the case, then I'm going to need to see some identification," he replied.

I went for my wallet, but I came up empty. My clutch—I'd left it with Maggie. My name tag—I'd dropped that into a trash can. Such screwups were typical Gloria.

"Miss?" inquired the guy. He was quickly becoming a jerk.

"You'd better let him through," I demanded, trying to sound forceful.

"I'm just doing my job," said the jerk.

"You know, that badge doesn't give you any real power," I said. "You're hotel security. You can't even carry a gun."

"That's it," said the jerk. He pulled a walkie-talkie off his belt. "Now, unless you can show me *your* ticket, then I'm going to have to throw both your asses out of here."

"How dare you?" I growled.

The jerk turned to Charlie threateningly. "What about you, kid? Care to get yourself in even more trouble?"

Shrugging, Charlie made a curious *eh* sound. Then he said, "She seems to be doing a good enough job for both of us."

Flipping on his headset, the jerk started talking to someone on the other end.

"Charlie," I said, "do something."

"What?"

"I don't know. *Something.*"

"I don't want to make things worse."

"They can't get worse," I said.

"I can't make it better."

"You can try."

"I leave in three days, Gloria."

I looked at him. All that mattered was now. "I don't care," I said. "Now do something!"

A smile of delight (the one I loved) crossed his face.

Then he sidled closer. His hand found mine. He squeezed.

Seconds later we were sprinting—past security, past the cocktail party, past my sister, and past the banquet hall on to God knows where, but where I didn't care.

It was the strangest thing. I didn't need to trespass. I had a ticket. I had more than that. I was introducing Bill Cosby in twenty minutes. But I didn't care. It didn't matter. I was running, and Charlie was beside me. And no one could stop us.

Not as long as we were together.

They never caught us, and by the time we ran out of breath, our marathon had ended back at the hotel's grand front entrance with its clean white awning and bushes trimmed with lights. Gasping, we collapsed on the bench beside the sliding doors. We sat in silence watching the handsome young valets taking keys for cash in their bright scarlet coats with gold buttons.

Neither of us spoke for what felt like forever. Instead, we leaned against each other, fingers entwined, and stayed like that for a long time. I don't know how long.

We didn't feel like waiting around for the guards to find

us, so we got up from the bench and wandered out past the driveway to the sidewalk. A soft neon glow radiated from two blocks down, an oasis of nightclubs, restaurants, and twenty-four-hour magazine stands. People clustered in small groups on the street corners. Taxis slowed down and sped up, swarming to the lights like moths. The energy of it all drew us in.

"Let's take a walk," I suggested. "We haven't had a pretty night in a while."

I meant "we" as in everyone, but it came out as if I meant the two of us. That would have been okay, too, because it was true.

Hand in hand, we strolled through the Washington evening. It was clear, and it was warm, and we had the glow of the streetlamps and stars to guide us.

ACKNOWLEDGMENTS

Some of this novel is true, meaning events actually happened to me. Some of it is a lie, meaning events are completely fabricated and possibly border on ridiculous. But despite being mostly fiction, *Freak Magnet* is about two very real people. Even as I worked on other projects, it was comforting to know that I would return to Gloria and Charlie at the end of the day. I adore these kids, for who they are and for who I imagined them becoming. Life is very hard, and I did not spare them the pain. I guess that was my way of treating them with respect and honesty.

Freak Magnet's also a tribute to the Washington DC area, a place that inspires a host of emotions, including love. I will forever feel at home in the neighborhoods of Arlington, Virginia, along the paths of the National Mall, and in the crowded boutiques of M Street. Revisiting them for this book was like flipping through a photo album of my time there, of living and working, and of falling for a DC girl.

On that note, I'd like to thank the one person who makes my writing career possible: my wife, Sarah Zogby. Without her endless support, I would have given up long ago. Because of you, I have achieved more than I ever imagined.

I'd like to thank my incredible editor, Farrin Jacobs, for taking my writing places it's never been before, and for trusting me enough to bring me aboard her crazy train. I learned more than I expected to. She has given me many reasons to be proud of this novel. I'd also like to thank my intrepid agent, Barry Goldblatt, who is forever toiling on my behalf and who sees a special, cozy place for me in all this YA craziness, even when I don't.

Heartfelt thanks to Margaret Carruthers and Richard Ash, who took time out of their busy lives to review the science portions of this novel. They make me look better, and smarter, than I have any right to be.

As always, I'd like to thank my families, the Auseons and the Zogbys, for their continued support, specifically my two wonderful daughters, Samara and Tess. And thanks to all my close friends and writing peers who have in one way or another played a part in the writing of *Freak Magnet*: the Big Huge Narrative crew of Zak Garriss, Tom Murphy, and Ben Schneider; Carmen Brock; Little Tony Cleveland; Ike Ellis; Lawrence Fels; Eddie Gamarra, and everyone at the Gotham Group; Gretchen Hirsch, Scott Neumyer; John-Paul Walton; Nell Whiting, Gregg Wilhelm, and M. T. Anderson, for always being someone I look to for clarity of vision.

**YOUNG
ADULT
FICTION
Auseon**

Auseon, Andrew.

Freak magnet